THE ABSOLUTELY AMAZING ADVENTURES OF AGENT AUGGIE SPINOZA

Steven Stickler

ISBN: 978-1470162870

Table of Contents

Preface

Dear reader,

What is revealed in these pages is of the utmost importance. It is not something to be skimmed over or considered lightly. It will require your full attention and all your powers of concentration. Even then, you should prepare to be shocked by what you learn. I, myself, was shaken by many of the details of this story. In fact, I considered destroying this manuscript as soon as it was completed, as I was not sure the world was ready to read this story.

Fortunately, my fellow agents convinced me that publication of this book was vitally important. Without their encouragement, and the actions many of them have taken to protect my life and my writing, I could not have continued. For, you see, writing books is not my primary occupation. Most of my friends think I'm a librarian, and it's true that I work at a library. But my primary job, the occupation to which I owe my utmost responsibility, the vocation for which I was born, is a classified secret known to only a select few. I can't even tell you, my faithful reader, what that job is. The most I can reveal, and I hope I am not revealing too much, is that I work with history.

It was in the course of performing the duties of my job (the precise nature of which I can't reveal) that I became aware of the story you are about to read. It took me several years to reconstruct and write using interviews and various documents and is, to the best of my abilities, an accurate picture of what actually happened.

Simply put, the topic of the story is this: our world is engulfed in a monumental battle. Few know about it. Fewer still participate in it. It is not a battle that is mentioned in newspapers or on the evening news, nor is it a battle that is taught in any school. But it is a fundamental struggle that has been raging for centuries and the outcome will determine the fate of the world in which we live.

This story will help you understand how the battle is being fought and why. What the story *won't* do is help you decide how to use that information once you have it. On this issue I'd advise the utmost caution and discretion. One can never be too careful.

Best of luck,
Special Agent Steven Stickler

Location: classified
Date: classified

Chapter 1: The Unraveling

Or, why you should always think twice (or even thrice!) before tugging on loose threads

Auggie Spinoza was not one of those kids who sat around wishing he could change the past. But now, as he sat in stunned silence surrounded by bitter cold and total darkness, he wished desperately for just one more chance to do things over.

He was scared, nervous, and tired.

Most of all, he was sorry. Sorry that he hadn't paused to think about what he was doing. Sorry that he hadn't told his parents what he discovered. Sorry—dreadfully, miserably, terrifyingly sorry—that he hadn't stayed in his bed, pulled the covers up to his chin, and gone to sleep when he had the chance.

If he could do it over again, he would do any of those things instead of what he actually did. But as much as any of us might want to change the past, none of us can. Life doesn't give us any do-overs. At least, that's what Auggie thought to himself as he sat there in the dark with his teeth chattering from the cold, his heart pounding with fear, and his body filled with a nervous trembling.

It all started with the hole in the curtain. He first noticed it the night before when he crawled behind the sofa looking for his toy light saber: a small, round hole the size of a pea. It blended so well with the pattern of the curtain that he could barely see it. He had probably looked at the curtains a million times without noticing it, perhaps because they had been there for so long and he was so familiar with the pattern—a sprinkling of randomly spaced brown circles and green dots on a creamy white background, like a bunch of big Cheerios and green M&Ms scattered on a white, sandy beach—that he had not looked closely at the curtains in years.

But he definitely noticed the curtains now. And he couldn't take his eyes off of that hole. It was behind the sofa, about a foot from the floor, right in the center of one of the brown circles. The only thing that made it look different from the centers of all the other brown circles was the frayed fabric at its edges and the utter darkness at its center, a darkness that made the shadows behind the sofa look like sunshine reflected off the ocean in comparison. Otherwise, it looked like just an ordinary hole in an ordinary curtain behind an ordinary sofa in an ordinary room.

As soon as he saw it, though, Auggie knew that it wasn't ordinary.

There was something special about it, something he could feel but not quite explain, a sense that it was a hole but more than *just* a hole; a feeling that it contained something both important and mysterious at the same time.

And then there was the tingling. Very slight, hard to notice, but definitely there: an electric, excited, ticklish tingling in his fingers and his toes. Sort of like the way his tongue felt the first time he put Pop-Rocks on it. Or the way his frozen fingers felt as he warmed them in front of the fireplace following a midwinter snowball fight.

He sat there for a minute staring at the hole, filled with a mixture of feelings and emotions he had never felt before. He was drawn to the hole and excited about it, but at the same time he was filled with a strange sort of nervousness, a feeling that if he wasn't scared, maybe he should be.

It seemed strange to him that a simple hole in a curtain could inspire such feelings, or that a kid like him—a kid who imagines himself battling droids, Orcs and Titans, a kid who was the first in his class to give an oral report on the Revolutionary War, a kid who played goalie against the Westside Cougars—would be the least bit nervous or scared when confronted with something so mundane.

It wasn't that Auggie felt he was any braver than any other kid. There were plenty of things that made him scared, and a lot more things that made him nervous. He was scared of spiders, for one thing, and of course he always felt nervous when he had to speak in front of large groups of people, especially when a bunch of kids he knew were in the audience watching him. Being nervous about those things made sense to him. Being nervous about a hole did not. Whether it made sense or not, though, that was the way he felt.

Clutching his toy light saber with one hand he slowly reached out and placed his other hand over the hole. What he felt surprised him: there was cold air coming from the hole, as if the window were open and the cold air from outside were blowing in. But when he pulled the curtain away from the wall to see what was behind it there was nothing there except the wall. And when he looked at the back of the curtain, he couldn't see the hole at all. Curious, he looked at the front of the curtain again. Sure enough, the hole was still there, though perhaps a bit smaller than he had first thought.

Thinking that maybe the hole was not visible on the back of the curtain because it was so small, he very carefully began to pull the frayed threads at the edge of the hole, slowly unraveling the fabric to make the hole bigger. The threads were strong and a bit sticky, but he pulled and pulled inch after inch of thread until the hole was about the size of a quarter. He knew that he had to work quickly and quietly, because his dad was just in the next room preparing dinner. He would not exactly be thrilled to find that Auggie was tearing a hole in the curtain.

Pausing first to take a deep breath and collect himself and his emotions, Auggie slowly put his right index finger through the hole as far as it would go.

What struck him immediately was the cold, like he had just put his finger in a tub of ice water. That and the sticky wet feeling of the edge of the hole, like the feeling of a fruit rollup or maybe a Popsicle before it gets licked. Keeping his finger all the way in the hole, Auggie stuck his head around to look at the back of the curtain, certain that he would see his finger poking through. But when he looked, he saw nothing. Nothing but the back of the curtain.

No finger.

No hole.

Nothing.

Auggie dropped his light saber and was about to grab the back of the curtain with his other hand when he heard his dad calling to him from the next room.

"Augs, time to get the table set for dinner, please."

Auggie quickly pulled his finger back out of the hole, grabbed his light saber, and darted from behind the sofa just in time to see his dad walking into the room.

"So your light saber ended up behind the sofa again, huh? Well, at least you know where to find it when it's lost. Let's get the table set," said his dad as he turned and walked back into the kitchen.

Whew, that was a close one, thought Auggie. *If dad had found me tearing a hole in the curtain, he would not have been happy.* But it was more than that. Auggie knew that if his dad had found the hole in the curtain, he would have told Auggie not to mess with it, to leave it alone, that he would fix it the next day. And Auggie did not want to leave it alone. And he certainly didn't want it to be fixed.

No, he wanted to spend more time investigating it. *Maybe after dinner*, Auggie thought as he walked into the kitchen, stopping once to glance back at the curtain, as if some secret would be revealed to him from just a glance.

Augustine. That was his name. Augustine Jeremy Spinoza. It was a long name, and too complicated for most kids his age. Most fourth graders were used to names that were one syllable long, or maybe two. But three syllables? In a name nobody had ever heard before? That's just too many. Plus, try yelling out "Augustine" if you want the ball in a basketball game. By the time you get the name out, you wouldn't be open any more.

He wasn't sure how he ended up with such a complicated and impractical name. His dad always claimed that his name was special, and he once started to tell Auggie some complicated story involving the names of famous authors and some other stuff that Auggie didn't really understand or didn't really feel like paying attention to at the time. His mom changed the subject whenever he asked her, almost like she was uncomfortable talking about it. So Auggie wasn't sure what the real story behind his name was.

Whatever the reason, even his parents had given up by now using his first name. Instead, they called him Auggie like most kids did. Or Augs. Or AJ. His little sister, who was still learning to talk, called him Uggs, like the boots.

He liked any of those names more than he liked the name Augustine, but that was his name and every time a new school year started that's the name the teacher would call him. So for the first few weeks of school it was always Augustine this and Augustine that, until eventually even his teacher got tired of that mouthful and started calling him Auggie just like everyone else did.

Auggie didn't spend the evening thinking about his name or where it came from, though. He spent the evening waiting. He waited through dinner while his mom and dad discussed their day, their plans for the weekend, how great the dinner was, blah, blah, blah. He waited after dinner as his dad sat on the sofa—yes, the very same sofa that sat in front of the curtains—reading his book, seeming to take forever, never getting up and leaving the room to give Auggie a chance to sneak behind the sofa and examine the curtain. It was as if he knew exactly what Auggie wanted to do and was intent on stopping him.

He waited and waited until finally it was his bedtime. He went upstairs and rushed through his bedtime routine. He brushed his teeth and set out his homework for the morning. Then he lay in bed with the light on, staring at his book and turning the pages without really reading it until finally it was time to turn off the light. He said goodnight to his mom and then lay there pretending to sleep but secretly waiting until everyone in the house was asleep so he could go back downstairs and look at the curtain.

He waited while his parents talked quietly downstairs, occasionally bursting out in laughter but then staying silent for what seemed like hours. He waited as his parents walked upstairs. He waited as they brushed their teeth. He waited as his dad went back downstairs to make sure he had locked all the doors. He waited as his parents lay in bed with their light on, reading and reading and reading. He waited as his parents finally turned their light out.

He waited and waited and waited.

Finally, mercifully, he could hear the unmistakable grinding snore of his dad, like a rusty hinge being opened and closed, opened and closed, opened and closed. He had never been so happy to hear that awful, irritating snore. He knew that if his mom had been awake, she would have been nudging his dad to stop the snoring, so he reasoned that she must have been asleep, too.

Climbing carefully and quietly out of his bed, Auggie shoved his feet into his slippers, wiggling his toes as they nestled into the soft, furry lining. From his nightstand he grabbed a headlamp he sometimes used for reading and strapped it onto his head. Slowly, and worried that with every step he would make a noise that would wake up one of his parents—maybe his ankle cracking, a floorboard creaking, or his slippers rustling against the carpet—he made his way down the stairs to the family room.

As he turned on his headlamp Auggie got that feeling again: the ticklish tingle in his fingers and toes, and with it this time the sense that the curtain was pulling him toward it. He crawled behind the sofa and aimed his headlamp at the curtain. He expected to see the hole pretty quickly, given that he had made it as large as a quarter only a few hours before. But he had to look very carefully and it took him a full minute to locate the hole. When he located the hole, he was surprised to find that it was no longer the size of a quarter. It was smaller, the size of a pea, as if it had slowly been shrinking as he waited upstairs.

He did not spend much time trying to figure out how this could be so.

He had work to do.

Taking a deep breath, Auggie reached out for the hole and began unraveling the fabric again. This time he did not go slowly. He hurried. Within a few minutes, the hole was big enough for him to put his fist through. But he kept unraveling. He unraveled and unraveled and unraveled.

Soon, the hole was as big as a basketball. But he kept unraveling, pulling and pulling at the threads as if opening a package, until the hole looked big enough for him to stick his head through, his shoulders through, and maybe even his entire body through.

Auggie quickly looked behind the curtain with his headlamp. Once again, no hole. How could it be that a hole the size of a beach ball on one side of the curtain would be invisible on the other side of the curtain?

This would have been the time to stop and think about such a question. Yes, this would have been a good time to pause for at least a few minutes or even a few hours before doing anything. Pause to breathe normally and let his mind think clearly, pause to think about what the smart thing to do was, maybe even pause to go get his parents and show them what he had found. Pause just to pause.

But Auggie did not pause. He could not pause. Pausing was the furthest thing from his mind. He felt excited and scared at the same time. But more than that, he felt the hole drawing him in, stronger than before, as if he were powerless to do anything except stick his head in it.

Without any second-guessing or even rational planning, that's exactly what he did. First his head, then his shoulders, then his arms and waist wiggled through the hole until he was resting his hands on the ground on the inside of the hole while resting his knees on the ground on the outside of the hole, feeling his knees against the soft, furry carpet and the frayed fabric of the curtain around his waist like a snug belt.

So just like that, there he was. The problem was, he had no idea where "there" was. All he knew at that moment was that he was cold. Very cold. Extremely cold. Cold like an icicle. Cold like the coldest snow at the top of Mt. Everest. Cold like Luke Skywalker on the ice planet Hoth. Cold like Edmund wandering in the woods of Narnia. Just plain cold.

It wasn't just cold, it was dark. Very dark. Extremely dark. Dark like the crawlspace under the house. Dark like the garage when no lights are on. Dark like the Mines of Moria. So dark that the light from his headlamp made no difference. Dark.

Auggie was about to crawl through the hole completely when something made him stop. It was a noise, faint at first but growing stronger and stronger until he soon realized that this was a familiar noise, a noise that he knew. It took him a few seconds to realize what it was: his alarm clock, beeping from the nightstand in his bedroom, telling him that it was time to get up.

Was it morning already? Had he really spent the whole night unraveling the curtain? Or had he spent more time climbing through the hole than he thought? Auggie didn't know. But he did know that if he did not get himself upstairs, soon everyone in the house would be awake and they would realize that he was downstairs. That would make them curious, because even though Auggie was always the first one out of bed in the morning, he was never the first one to come downstairs. That was usually one of his parents.

Normally Auggie wouldn't care if his parents were curious. But in this case he worried that if they got curious enough they might just decide to look around the family room, maybe even to look behind the sofa. And if they decided to look behind the sofa he knew what they would see: a giant hole in the curtain.

He couldn't have that. If they saw it they would fix it. And he wasn't ready to have it fixed.

So Auggie quickly pulled himself out of the hole. First his waist and his shoulders then his arms and his head. Once he was out, he took his slippers off and held them in his hands so that he could walk quietly up the stairs, as fast as he could go without making noise, down the hallway to his room where he clicked off his alarm just as he had done hundreds of other times on hundreds of other ordinary mornings to start hundreds of other ordinary days. As he climbed in his bed, though, Auggie knew that this had been no ordinary morning, and he didn't expect that this would be like any other ordinary day.

About that, at least, Auggie was entirely correct: it would not be an ordinary day.

He spent the entire day in a distracted daze. He brushed his teeth but forgot to use toothpaste. He ate a bagel and banana for breakfast but then forgot that he had eaten breakfast and ate another bagel and banana. When the bus got to school, his friend Oliver had to elbow him in the ribs to remind him to get off the bus. He left his backpack on when he sat down at his desk. He got up to go to the bathroom but ended up in a custodian's closet instead.

The whole day was like that. He could not concentrate at all, thinking instead about the hole in the curtain and planning what he would do that night after everyone in the house was asleep.

Throughout the entire day, Auggie saw tiny holes everywhere he looked. In the ceiling tiles in his classroom. In the bulletin board in the hallway. In the play structure at recess. Even in the toe of Mrs. Peppersnell's red sneaker. There were holes everywhere.

He made it through the day, but barely. School, the bus ride home, snack, homework, piano lesson, soccer practice: all of these he went through without actually experiencing them until finally he was home, it was dinner time, and all he had to do was wait through a normal, uneventful evening.

Or so he thought.

Auggie had been so excited by the events of the prior evening, and so distracted throughout the entire day that he had completely forgotten an important fact which at any other time would have captivated his attention: tomorrow was his birthday. That simple fact alone, on any other day, would have been all Auggie could have thought about. What's more, this wasn't just any birthday; it was his tenth birthday, a milestone which his parents had been hinting for years would be the most significant he would ever experience. It would, they always told him, be the birthday of all birthdays, the one he would remember for years and years.

Normally on the day before his birthday he searched the house for presents, lifting and shaking and pressing and even smelling any that he found, trying to decipher their contents. But he had been so distracted by the hole in the curtain that not only had he forgotten to look for presents, he had forgotten completely that tomorrow was his birthday.

It wasn't until he walked into the dining room for dinner and saw a stack of birthday presents on the center of the table that he remembered the significance of the date. It was an impressive stack of presents, each of them wrapped in dull blue and green wrapping paper except for one, the one on top, the one that had the unmistakable shape and size of a hardcover book, the one that was wrapped in the most exquisite, shiny, gold foil that Auggie had ever seen.

"That one on top is pretty special. I think we'll have you open that one last. You'll never be able to guess what's inside, so I wouldn't bother trying." His mother grinned and winked at him as she carried the plates over to the table. "Why don't you help me set the table so we can eat? I'm starving."

Auggie had to admit that he was hungry, too. It was something other than hunger, though, that made him look forward to sitting down to eat dinner: he was anxious to get back to the curtain, and he knew that once dinner was over he would be that much closer to nighttime, when he could sneak back downstairs to explore the hole in the curtain.

No sooner did his family sit down at the table for dinner, though, than there was a loud and persistent knock at the door followed by several rings of the doorbell.

"I wonder what the emergency is," asked his dad sarcastically as he got up to answer the door. Auggie followed, curious to see who it was.

There, in the doorway, was a tall man with a suitcase. He had a narrow, coyote-like face, with a chin that jutted out far below his mouth and sharp cheekbones underlining his eyes so that from the front his face looked like a small triangle inside a large triangle with two eyes on top, and all of it topped off by straight shiny black hair that looked like it could use a good wash. Auggie thought there was something shifty and suspicious about his eyes, especially the way the eyelids narrowed when the man talked.

"Hi, sorry to bother you but I'm with the phone

company and we're having trouble with the phones in the area. I just need to come in and check your phone. Only take a minute, then I'll be out of your way." The man narrowed his eyes and looked past Auggie and his dad into the house behind them. It was only then that Auggie noticed his jacket. It was a navy blue cotton work jacket with a patch on the left chest that had the phone company logo on it. And when Auggie looked closer at the suitcase he could see that it was actually a bag of tools.

"Okay, we're just sitting down to dinner but if it'll be quick you're welcome to come on in," replied Auggie's dad as he showed the man inside.

Before Auggie's dad had even shut the door behind him, the man had walked inside and was already moving into the family room, straight for the sofa, directly toward the hole in the curtain. It was as if he knew exactly what was there and was planning to show Auggie's entire family.

Auggie was too far behind him to stop him.

Great, thought Auggie, *he is going to look behind the sofa and everyone will see the giant hole in the curtain. Then they'll all look at me and I'll have to explain what I did and why I did it, and I can't really explain that because I don't really know why. If I try to explain that thing about the cold on the other side, about how the hole and the things stuck in it weren't visible from the other side, about how the hole seemed to shrink like it was repairing itself, they'll think I'm crazy*, he thought. *Then they'll fix the hole.*

Just as Auggie was thinking his secret would be revealed, though, his dad lunged forward, darting between the man and the sofa like he was a goalie defending a goal. Auggie hadn't seen his dad move that fast since, well...ever. In fact, he hadn't ever really seen his dad move fast at all for any reason. But he sure moved fast now, and his speed was enough to make the man quickly halt.

[13]

"The phone isn't in here. It's over there," said Auggie's dad sternly as he pointed toward the kitchen.

The man with the coyote-like face and shifty, suspicious eyes paused for a moment, looking first at Auggie and then at his dad, narrowing his eyes a bit as if straining to decide what to do. He glanced slowly at the phone in the kitchen then gradually turned his head till his gaze settled on the stack of birthday presents sitting on the dining table.

For now, Auggie wasn't thinking about the anticipation of opening his presents, or even wondering what was inside them. In fact, he wasn't looking at the birthday presents at all. He was watching the man with the coyote-like face—or, as Auggie started thinking of him, Mr. Coyote—as his gaze rested on the birthday present wrapped in shiny, gold foil. In that gaze and the narrowed eyelids that surrounded it, Auggie could sense something like recognition. It was as if Mr. Coyote knew what was in the package and was trying to decide what he should do about it. He seemed about to move toward the present when Auggie's dad interrupted him. "What, exactly, is the matter with the phones?"

Something about the tone of his dad's voice, a steely sternness Auggie had never heard before, seemed to jar Mr. Coyote into attention. He looked again at Auggie's dad, fixed his gaze for just a moment, and then turned slowly around, glanced at the phone in the kitchen, and said, "actually it doesn't look like there's any problem with that phone. I think I can be going." With that, he walked quickly out the front door, down the front step, and into his utility van. By the time Auggie's dad had locked the front door, Mr. Coyote had driven away.

"Some repairman!" snorted his dad as they walked back into the kitchen. "Seemed like he was engaged in some sort of trickery, didn't it?"

"It sure did," replied Auggie's mother from the other side of the dinner table. "Whatever it was, it didn't seem like the truth, that's for sure."

As Auggie and his dad returned to the dinner table, Auggie noticed his parents exchange a knowing glance. He wondered why. Did they know something about Mr. Coyote? Like maybe who he was or why he was there? Did they know about the hole in the curtain, too? Is that why his dad had moved so quickly?

Whatever they might have known, Auggie did not have time to think about it just then.

All he could think about was how close his secret had come to being revealed. Well, he could think about that, and also about how strange and creepy the telephone man had seemed. Why did he walk straight toward the sofa? And why did he leave right away when they showed him where the phone was? And if there was a problem with all the phones in their neighborhood, why had he driven away after leaving their house? Come to think of it, why had his dad chosen that precise moment to reveal his previously hidden quickness? And how had he known to jump right in front of the sofa?

Auggie didn't know the answer to any of these questions, and he really didn't spend a lot of time thinking about them. What he was really thinking about was that hole.

The rest of the night was not unusual. In fact, it was just like the night before. He waited through dinner, waited while his dad read on the sofa, waited while he went through his bedtime routine, waited after he turned off his light, waited as his parents talked downstairs, waited as they brushed their teeth, waited while his dad went downstairs to lock all the doors, waited while his parents read with their light on, waited after they turned their light off, waited until, once again, he could hear his dad's familiar, comforting snore.

This time he was ready.

Quickly but quietly, he slipped out of bed and grabbed his headlamp from the nightstand. From his closet, he grabbed his warm socks and snow pants. From his bookshelf he grabbed his video camera. *This time,* he thought to himself, *I'll capture everything I see on video. That way I can show my parents and my friends.* Confident that he was well-prepared, he headed quietly downstairs, careful again to avoid the rustle of feet, the squeaking of floor, and now the bristly nylon rustle of his snow pants clutched in one arm.

Now, in most houses it is not a challenge to walk down the stairs quietly. But Auggie's house was not the same as most houses. For one thing, it was built in 1760. It was an old Victorian house in Cambridge, Massachusetts just down the street from Harvard University. His parents had bought it just before he was born and had spent years fixing it up.

That was the other unique thing about their house: instead of hiring professional craftsmen to fix their house, his parents had fixed it up themselves. They didn't hire an electrician to fix the wiring; they fixed it themselves. They didn't hire a plumber to replace all the plumbing; they replaced it themselves. Most importantly to Auggie at this point, however, was the fact that they didn't hire a carpenter who knew how to make the floorboards stop squeaking. Instead, Auggie's dad had spent the last 10 years pounding a nail into the floor anyplace he heard a squeak. It was not a particularly effective technique.

And so Auggie descended the stairway carefully, on tiptoes, worried with each step that he might produce a parent-awakening squeak.

When he arrived downstairs, he turned on his headlamp and walked past the family room to the utility room. There, he sat on the floor and slipped his socks on, then his snow pants, followed by his parka. From the shoe cabinet he reached out his snow boots, stocking hat, and gloves that had been stored there since the previous winter. He had vivid memories of the chilling cold contained within the hole in the curtain, and this time he planned to be prepared for it.

Once he had all that put on—the shoes a bit tight because his feet had grown since he last wore them, the parka big and bulky, and the stocking hat scratchy against his forehead—he marched back into the family room and knelt down behind the sofa, feeling once again a ticklish tingle in his fingers and toes.

He should not have been surprised at what he saw, but he was. The hole was still there, but it was not as big as a beach ball anymore, it wasn't as big as a basketball, and it was not even as big as his fist. It had shrunk again, to about the size of a quarter.

Auggie knew he could not waste any time. Setting his video camera on the ground, he pulled frantically at the thread, unraveling the fabric as quickly as he could until, in what seemed like no time at all, the hole was as big as a beach ball once again.

He took a deep breath, made sure his headlamp was on its brightest setting, and stuck both of his arms, then his head, and finally his shoulders through the hole, resting his hands on the ground on the other side. Feeling the rustle of his nylon parka and snow pants against the curtain,

Auggie gradually worked the rest of his body through the hole until his entire body—from his glove covered fingers to his snow boot wearing feet—was in the cold darkness on the other side of the curtain.

Auggie wasn't sure what he had expected, but it wasn't this. He was sitting in total darkness. He felt a bone-chilling, teeth-chattering, skin-numbing cold. And even with his headlamp he could see nothing at all. One thing he did know was that he wasn't in his house anymore, and he wasn't in his backyard, either. No, this was someplace completely different.

He started to reach back for his video camera but instead of the openness of the hole he had just crawled through, his arm hit something. It was something solid, like a rock or a wall. Auggie reached and reached, moving his hands around in space frantically trying to find the hole again, but all he could feel behind him was a solid, immovable wall.

The hole had disappeared behind him.

It was right then and right there that Auggie wished he could go back and change things. But as far as he knew, he couldn't. Wherever he was, he was stuck there.

This stark, scary fact had barely registered in Auggie's brain when he heard a gentle voice in the darkness. "Hello, is someone there?"

Chapter 2: The Secret
*Or, why you never really know
as much as you think you know*

Auggie wasn't sure what to do. He was still a little bit dazed from crawling through the hole, a little bit shocked by the fact that it had disappeared behind him, and more than a little bit scared about the fact that he was suddenly in a very different place that felt not at all like home. And now, on top of all of that, there was a voice coming from the darkness.

It wasn't that the voice was threatening. In fact it was gentle and even a little bit familiar, though he was pretty sure he had never heard it before. And it was a girl's voice so really he shouldn't have been all that afraid. Still, he was a bit nervous and uncertain. He had no idea where he was, he had no idea who the voice belonged to, and he was already wishing that he had paused to think about what he was doing before he crawled through the hole.

He felt like crawling back into the hole, running back upstairs, taking off his snow boots, his snow pants, his parka, and his stocking hat and jumping back into bed. But that wasn't an option. The hole wasn't there. So he sat there in the darkness for a few seconds, holding so still that he didn't even breathe.

Maybe if I hold still for long enough, thought Auggie, *she won't know I'm here and she'll go away.*

"You know, I can see you. You're wearing a headlamp. And if I'm not mistaken you have it set to the brightest setting. If you really want to hide, you might want to turn that off," whispered the voice in a kind but obviously teasing tone. "Anyway, my name is Emily. My friends call me Em. What's your name?"

Auggie blushed in the darkness and blurted out a greeting. "I'm Auggie. Where am I?"

"I wouldn't know any better than you," laughed Emily. "We never know where we are when we first get there. You know we won't find that out until—"

Auggie felt Emily clutch his arm just above the elbow. "Wait a second, did you say Auggie? As in Augustine? As in Augustine Jeremy Spinoza?"

"Y-y-yes," said Auggie, wondering how she could possibly know his whole name. Most of his friends didn't even know his whole name. Most of his teachers didn't know his whole name. The librarian he saw almost every day at school, who always gave him a bright smile and a "good morning, Auggie," like she had been waiting all morning just for him, didn't even know his whole name. His soccer coach didn't even know his whole name. How could this stranger in the dark know his whole name? And what did she mean when she said 'we never know where we are when we first get there'? Did she crawl through a curtain to get there just like he did? Had she done this before? Did she know how he could get back home?

Auggie wanted to ask her all these things and more, but he started with what seemed most pressing and, he thought, simple: "You know my name?"

"Oh, of course I know your name. Most of us do. That's what being the son of two agents will do for you, especially when they are the only two agents in all of history to get married."

"Wait a second, you know my parents, too? And what do you mean 'agents'?"

"You know, agents of the I.A.I.P.H." Emily explained with an exasperated tone, "and of course I know them. Well, I don't actually *know* them. It's not like I've ever met them or anything. But I've heard all about them. And I've seen their pictures, of course. They're legends. L-E-G-E-N-D-S," she spelled out the last word, as if maybe she had forgotten where she was and thought she was in a spelling bee.

Then she continued, "they've been retired now for quite a few years, of course, probably since about the time you were born. But all of the other agents still talk about them. And I think they still have the most visited wall at the agents Hall of Fame in London. I know it was sure crowded when my parents took me there. I could barely get close enough to see their pictures, and couldn't get close enough to read the details of their missions."

Auggie sat there in stunned, confused silence. Surely she was mistaken. *His* parents? *Agents? Legends? Missions?*

He thought for a moment about his parents. There was his dad, who owned and operated a rare bookshop that, as far as Auggie could tell, never had any customers. His dad, who spent most of his day leafing through the pages of dusty old books and manuscripts and most of his evenings reading or writing about stuff that was so boring that Auggie didn't even want to try to understand it. His dad, who had business cards that said "Chief Bookworm". His dad, who Auggie had never seen move faster than a slow stroll until today, and who was always happy to play or hike or swim, but always joked that he was hardly agile enough to get out of the car.

And then there was his mom, squirreled away most days in her office there at the University archives where she was the Chief Archivist, surrounded by old letters and unpublished manuscripts, sort of like a librarian for dusty old papers from centuries ago that hardly anyone ever wanted to read. His mom, who didn't spend her free time practicing karate or rock climbing, but rather shopping for antiques and organic turnips. His mom, who spoke so quietly that she couldn't even be heard if there was a light breeze blowing outside, as if she thought the entire world was a library and she needed to keep her voice down.

His parents, *these* parents—who if Auggie had to choose one word to describe besides "kind"or "nice" might be "meek"—*Agents*?

Auggie couldn't imagine this. But then, he thought, there were a lot of things that he couldn't imagine, like crawling through a hole in the curtain and ending up in a completely different place talking to somebody he'd never met before, somebody who knew his name, somebody who knew a lot more about him and where they were and what had happened than he did.

Auggie tried to organize his thoughts. He had many questions, but didn't know where to start. So, he started with the most obvious question of all: "Agents of what, exactly?"

"You know. Agents of the I.A.I.P.H."

"The I.A.I-*what*?"

"The I.A.I.P.H., of course. You know, the International Association for the Investigation and Preservation of History? Boy, you sure didn't read your Agent Orientation Manual very carefully, did you?"

"What Agent Orientation Manual? What are you talking about?"

"Didn't you get it for your 10th birthday? That's when most of us get it. Hard to travel through history without having read that manual. It explains everything."

It took a minute for this to register in Auggie's head. A manual? One that he was supposed to get on his 10th birthday?

Then it hit him: that's what was in the shiny gold foil package sitting on the kitchen counter, the one on the top of the stack of presents, the one that Mr. Coyote had looked at so carefully.

He was about to tell Emily that he hadn't actually turned 10 yet, that his birthday wasn't until tomorrow, when she said in an urgent, hushed whisper, "Shhhh, someone's coming!"

Auggie heard the loud screeching of hinges and suddenly everything went from dark to light in an instant. Someone had opened a large door at the opposite end of the room and bright sunlight suddenly filled the entire room, making Auggie squint.

He felt Emily whisper in his ear. "We have to move. Follow me."

As he felt her pulling him behind her, Auggie noticed that they were in some kind of room, like a garage or warehouse. The floors were made of muddy dirt and puddles of water lay scattered around the room. The walls, as far as he could see, were made of old splintered wood, like he remembered seeing in his grandfather's old shed. Auggie looked along the walls and saw drawings of birds and maps of islands. He saw stacks and stacks of glass jars filled with dried plants, rocks, and what looked like bird beaks. He saw plants and flowers hanging from the ceiling. He saw skeletons of birds and other small animals spread out on tables. He saw barnacles and coral and fish skeletons stacked on shelves. In the corner of the room he saw a butterfly net and an old fashioned fishing pole.

Emily pulled him between a storage cabinet and the

[23]

wall just as they heard the loud scuffle of feet and two men entered the room through the doorway that had just opened.

Auggie could see only one of them at first: a small, balding man wearing black pants and a gray suit coat over a checkered black and white vest. When the man turned his face toward the light Auggie could see that he wore small round glasses over his eyes and had a full black beard with streaks of gray hair running through it. He looked vaguely familiar to Auggie, but Auggie wasn't sure why.

Auggie couldn't make out the second man at first, because one of the machines was blocking his view. But just as Auggie was about to look around the rest of the room to try to figure out where they were, the man walked across the room to the exact spot where they had been sitting and Auggie caught a full glimpse of his face in the bright light.

What he saw sent chills through his whole body.

There (wherever there was) in front of him was the last person he expected to see.

Well, maybe not the last person.

He wouldn't have expected to see his gym teacher there. And he wouldn't have expected to see his friend Oliver there. He really wouldn't have expected to see his neighbor, Mr. Ruttulio, there either. But he would rather have seen any of them than the person he actually saw, because standing there in front of him, in muddy overalls and a wide-brim hat was the phone repairman, the man with the coyote-like face, Mr. Coyote.

The two men took turns bending and looking into a microscope on the other side of the room. Mr. Coyote seemed to be trying to convince the other man of something. He kept looking into the microscope and pointing to some papers he had spread out on the table. At one point he even walked over to the wall and pointed wildly to one of the drawings that looked like a family tree, except for birds. But the other man kept shaking his head, apparently unconvinced of whatever Mr. Coyote was trying to tell him.

Eventually they finished and both men walked toward the door. Just as he was closing the door behind him, though, Mr. Coyote turned and came back in to the room as if he had forgotten something. He walked directly to the wall where Auggie and Emily had been sitting only moments before. He placed his hands against the wall and moved them up and down and across, from the floor to as high as he could reach. Then he turned and bent over what looked like a pile of blankets in front of the wall.

But when he lifted the top blanket, Auggie could see that it was not a pile of blankets at all. It was some kind of machine. There were at least five bright yellow oblong cylinders, kind of like the tanks Auggie had seen scuba divers using. They were all strapped together and each had a black rubber hose coming out the top. Mr. Coyote adjusted some sort of dial on one of the tanks. Then he quickly covered the machine up again until it looked like a pile of blankets. And then he left, closing the squeaky door behind him and leaving Auggie and Emily in total darkness.

"Quick, we have to follow them." Emily tugged at his arm.

"I just want to look at that machine he was covering up," Auggie replied. What he really wanted to do was find that hole, crawl back through it, walk upstairs, and crawl into bed.

"We don't have time. Anyway, it's just a cold machine.

[25]

Makes the holes close faster. They do that to try to keep agents from crawling through. They figured that one out on their own. Well, not about the cold. We've known about that ever since the first agents traveled to the North Pole. The holes closed up on them in just a few hours. But we never thought to make a machine for closing the holes. Leave it to the Time Vultures. They are inventive, I'll give them that. Let's go."

Auggie had no idea what she was talking about. We? They? Time Vultures? But there was no time to ask now, because Emily was already opening the door with the rusty hinges. Auggie followed her outside.

They emerged from the doorway in full daylight on a road of dirt and pebbles. Auggie turned to look at the building. It was a simple wooden building with a large door on the front of it. It had been painted white with black trim at one point, but now most of the paint was flaking off, revealing weathered and cracked gray wood. A faded sign hung above the door: "Down Blacksmith".

They were in some sort of town, but it was not like any town Auggie had ever been in before. The road was not paved, there were no sidewalks, and there weren't any cars. Instead, there was a road made of dirt and stones and lined with several one-story buildings. Auggie could make out the lettering on only a few of them: "bakery" and "post office". Along the side of the street across from them was a horse and buggy, and further up the street Auggie could see two horses pulling a large wagon.

Emily grabbed him by the arm. "Come on. They went this way. And you can probably lose that headlamp now. Don't want to attract too much attention."

Auggie had forgotten that he was still wearing his headlamp. He slipped it off his head and stuffed it into the

[26]

pocket of his parka.

Up the street about 100 feet Auggie could see the two men walking. Auggie and Emily began walking in their direction, hanging back far enough that they wouldn't be noticed. Suddenly the two men stopped and faced each other. They seemed to be having a disagreement of some sort. Before they got too close, Auggie and Emily stopped along the side of the street, trying hard to look inconspicuous.

It's now or never, thought Auggie, *I need to get some answers.*

He looked straight at Emily, noticing her for the first time. She seemed a bit older than him, but about the same height. She had straight black hair that hung down to her shoulders. Her nose and cheeks were covered with freckles. She wore a simple white T-shirt with jeans and sneakers. Over her shoulder, she carried a small blue backpack.

Auggie reached up and rubbed his head. "So, first of all I'm not 10. I don't turn 10 until tomorrow. And second of all, I have no idea where we are or what is going on."

And then he told her more. He told her about the curtain and the hole. He told her about waiting and waiting for his parents to fall asleep. He told her about the telephone repairman that looked like a coyote, about how he thought one of the two men was the very same man. He told her about the birthday present wrapped in gold foil. He told her about how he crawled through the hole in the curtain, about how shocked he was by the darkness and cold. He told her a lot of things, things that he wasn't sure mattered but that he felt like he should tell her. Like how much he liked to read, and about the time that he got up in front of the whole school in an assembly to give a speech even though he was so nervous and scared that his head felt dizzy and his stomach felt like it had strings attached pulling it in all different directions.

Emily seemed stunned. "Wait, so your parents haven't told you anything? Nothing about the holes in time? The Great Battle Over Time and History? The Grand Conspiracy? Any of this ringing any bells? "

Auggie gave her a blank stare and shook his head.

Emily let out a long sigh. "Okay, we don't have much time, so I'll give you a short version. We'll have to fill in the blanks later. Here's the deal: that hole you just crawled through was a hole in time and space. When you crawled through it you moved from your time and place to whenever and wherever we are now."

"And where is that?"

Auggie watched Emily roll her eyes in exasperation. "Like I said, we never know where or when we are when we first get there. I don't completely understand how it works. I tried to get my dad to explain it to me once. He told me time is kind of like a long train moving along a winding track that never ends. The front of the train is like the beginning of time, and cars are always being added to the end of the train just like new days are always happening. So if you walked from the very front of the train to the very back of the train you would see all of history. Now, most people live their lives in only one car of this train and they experience their own time as it happens. They can't walk from one train car to the other, from one part of history to another part of history. But some of us are different. Some of us get the chance to move from our own part of history to another part of history. Aren't we lucky? L-U-C-K-Y."

Emily spelled out the last word again. Auggie wasn't sure why she kept doing that. Did she think he didn't know how to spell? Did she even know she was doing it? Maybe it was some sort of disease or nervous habit. Whatever the case, Auggie didn't think this was the time to ask her about it. He reached both hands up to rub the hair on his head vigorously several times, the way he did when confronted with a math problem he didn't understand. "So...how does that work?"

Emily chuckled. "Okay, so that is a way more complicated question than we have time for me to answer. Just look at it this way: that train I was talking about travels along this track that never ends. It twists and winds and curves and doubles back. Every once in a while, one part of the track comes so close to another part of the track that one part of the train nearly touches another part of the train. When that happens, it's like two periods of history are almost touching. I can't tell you why, but that's when the holes appear. And the holes let us crawl from one part of history into another. But it's not like we know in advance what part of history we're going to crawl into—we don't have a map of the train track or anything, and we certainly don't have a time-space GPS."

They were standing in front of the town's bakery now, waiting as the two men stood up the street talking. Auggie's nostrils could smell the sour sweet scent of freshly baked sourdough bread mixed with the fruity aroma of blackberry pie. Parked along the curb was a cart filled with burlap sacks, each covered with a dusty white layering of flour. A large man wearing a red apron was carrying the sacks one by one, trip after trip, from the cart into the bakery.

Auggie cleared his throat. "So can I get home through that hole I just used? It seems like it's gone."

Emily shook her head and then nodded. "No and yes.

The holes usually don't stay open for more than a day. It's like they grow shut. And the cold machine only makes them shut faster. So that hole is probably gone by now. But there will be others. Whenever one hole closes another one opens up. Not right away, but soon. But the thing is, the holes can only open up for as long as the time we are in now is next to the time we came from. Once the two parts of time aren't next to each other anymore, we are stuck. That's why once we've crawled through time, we have to hurry up and complete our mission so we can get back home."

"So how do I find one of those other holes?"

"Well, it's more like they find you. They're out there, but you probably won't notice them until you get that feeling. You know, the tingling? When you feel that, you'll know there is a hole nearby. And you should find it fast and crawl through, because it might not be there for long. Oh, and the other thing is: each hole only works for a particular person. The hole that works for you won't work for me. It's like they are custom made."

Just as Emily finished, Auggie and Emily looked over to where the two men had been standing. Emily gasped. Mr. Coyote had vanished. The other man had crossed the street and was walking away from them, toward the edge of town. They hurried to follow him.

They followed as he walked past the church and the post office, they followed as he continued along the road leading out of town, and they followed as the wide road became a narrow dirt lane, bordered by woods on the left and open pastures on the right. They followed him for what seemed like miles, accompanied the entire time by the gentle swish-swish rustling sound of Auggie's snow pants.

They followed and followed and followed.

As they walked, Emily began to explain what was going on. For starters, her name was Emily Niccolo Emerson and she was 12 years old. Her dad called her Em-N-Em ("you know, M&M, like the candy," she said with a wink). She had been traveling through time for a few years now and had completed dozens of missions.

That part was easy to understand. It was when she started explaining time travel and the Great Battle Over Time and History that Auggie started to get confused.

"I don't know the whole history of it and everything like that," she said, "but I do know that the battle has been going on for centuries, since shortly after people started crawling through time."

Centuries and centuries ago, she told him, there were people just like them traveling through time. Just as Auggie had, these people would find holes and crawl through them into the past. Once there, they would observe and take notes and then return to their own time with a deeper understanding of history. They called themselves Time Watchers.

The very first Time Watchers obeyed a simple rule: watch history, but don't try to change it. The reason was simple. They believed that once they started messing around with their past, they would make unpredictable changes in their present.

Sounds like an easy rule to follow, but it really wasn't. There were always bad things happening in history, things they wished they could change. So it was always tempting to make small changes to eliminate suffering or stop bad things from happening. Most of the Time Watchers resisted this temptation because they knew that tinkering with history could be dangerous.

But it didn't take long before some of the Time

Watchers stopped following the rule. And they did it for selfish reasons: they thought they could figure out how making small changes in history would make them more powerful in the present. Some of them had grand ambitions. They hoped to someday rule the entire world simply by controlling history. They came to be called Time Vultures because they tried to take advantage of their ability to crawl through history.

"I don't understand," said Auggie, "hasn't history already happened? How can it be changed?"

"Well, I'm no physicist, but here's the way my parents explained it to me: while it's happening, history can take many different courses; nothing in history *had* to happen the way it did at the time. Once it has happened, though, history becomes frozen into our unchanging past. But when we crawl through time, we are experiencing somebody else's present. So what we see isn't history, or even the past yet, because technically it hasn't really happened yet. So the problem is, if we make changes while we're here we'll end up making changes in our present, too."

"Oh, boy." Auggie shook his head and looked up at the sky.

"Yeah, I know. Big responsibility." Emily nodded her head in understanding. "So anyway, ever since the first Time Vultures started trying to change history, a battle has been raging between the two sides, with one side trying to protect history and the other side trying to change it. The Time Watchers versus the Time Vultures. We are Time Watchers. We are on the side that's trying to protect history. We are the good guys."

"But you said before that we are agents. What are we agents of? And who do we work for?"

"Oh yeah, that's the most important part," replied Emily. "That all started way back at the beginning. As soon as the Time Vultures started trying to change history, the rest of the Time Watchers knew they needed to get organized. So they set up an organization called the International Association for the Investigation and Preservation of History, the I.A.I.P.H. It's been around for as long as anyone can remember. That's who we work for. We crawl through time trying to stop Time Vultures from changing history. That's probably why your Mr. Coyote is here. He's probably a Time Vulture. He's probably trying to change something that happened here in this time. We are here to stop him."

"But how, exactly, do we battle the Time Vultures? What kind of weapons do we use?" Auggie imagined himself with a light saber or maybe a sword, battling Mr. Coyote in the swirling winds of a hurricane, atop some sort of tank or other kind of war machine, teetering on the edge of a cliff.

Emily shook her head. "No, it's not that kind of battle at all. It's more like we use our brains. The Time Vultures go back in time and try to change history by persuading people to change their minds about what they want to do. We just try to keep people from being persuaded to do the wrong thing. So, for example, I had one mission where a Time Vulture was trying to persuade General Washington to surrender at Valley Forge. I persuaded him to stick with his plan. That was a very successful mission."

According to Emily, the battle had been going on for centuries, and most of the time agents of the I.A.I.P.H. were successful in completing their missions and preventing the Time Vultures from changing history. But not always.

"You've heard of Attila the Hun?" asked Emily.

Auggie hadn't, but he nodded anyway.

"Yeah, that was our fault. Some Time Vulture taught a kid some dangerous leadership skills. We weren't able to stop him. Kind of backfired on them, though. Ended up creating a war-hungry marauder that caused all kinds of suffering, even for Time Vultures. Taught all of us an important lesson: no matter how smart you think you are, changing history is dangerous."

Auggie was starting to feel like he was in history class. Time Watchers. Time Vultures. Great Battle Over Time and History. This was a lot for him to try to understand, but he kept nodding his head as Emily continued.

"So this battle had been going on for many centuries and then, about 50 years ago, the Time Vultures said they were ready to stop changing history. They even offered to come to the headquarters of the I.A.I.P.H. to sign an agreement saying that they would stop interfering in history."

"Cool," Auggie said because he couldn't think of anything else to say.

"Yeah, everyone was really relieved. So all the agents and Time Vultures gathered together at the I.A.I.P.H. headquarters and signed an agreement saying that none of them would try to interfere in history. Of course, all of the agents were really excited about the battle being over. They felt like they had achieved a great victory, and that they didn't have to worry about protecting history any longer. They were even preparing to hold a giant celebration. Until they realized it was all a trick."

"A trick? What kind of a trick?"

"Well, we didn't figure this out until years later, but those Time Vultures never intended to honor the

[34]

agreement that they signed. The real reason that they wanted everyone to sign the agreement was because—hey, it looks like he's stopping. I'll have to tell you the rest later. DON'T LET ME FORGET!"

Sure enough, the man had stopped momentarily before turning up a small dirt pathway leading to a large white house surrounded on all sides by lawns and flower gardens. Emily and Auggie rushed toward the entrance to the pathway, where they stopped at a small white sign with black letters that read "Down House."

Auggie felt like he had been hit by lightning. He knew exactly where they were. He remembered this from his third-grade class project. Down House was the house that the scientist Charles Darwin lived and worked in. It was in England, just outside London. This is where he conducted many of his experiments and where he wrote most of his papers and books. That must have been why the man looked vaguely familiar to Auggie. It must have been Charles Darwin himself.

But if that was Charles Darwin, Auggie thought to himself, *then that would mean that we are in the nineteenth century*. Judging from Darwin's age and appearance, Auggie guessed that it was sometime in the 1850s. That was about 150 years before Auggie was even born.

Auggie was about to tell Emily all of this when they were both startled by a voice from behind them. "Hey, where did you two come from?"

Chapter 3: The Scientist

Or, why it is very important to remember what you learn in school

Emily and Auggie whirled around to see a boy about their age standing in the road. He was about the same height as Auggie, with shiny, light brown hair and a round face filled with dozens of tiny freckles. He was wearing a long-sleeved white button-down shirt and tan mud-covered pants that ended between his knees and ankles, and on his feet he wore not the sneakers or sandals so common among Auggie's friends but instead brown leather shoes that looked a lot like Auggie's dress shoes except for the fact that they were covered with mud.

Auggie noticed all these things about him without really thinking about it, because all of his attention was focused on the boy's eyes. There was something about those eyes, something familiar, almost as if they had known Auggie forever and knew exactly what he was thinking right now. Unlike Mr. Coyote's eyes, though, these eyes seemed friendly, trustworthy, and kind. Just the eyes alone made Auggie feel comfortable and relaxed.

"Did you come from town? Is there anyone with you?" There was a kind of good-natured teasing suspicion in the boy's voice, as if he knew they were trying to get away with something.

Auggie was too surprised to respond, but Emily was ready with a reply: "Yep, we walked from town. Our parents told us we could go exploring so that's what we're doing. I'm Emily. This is Auggie. What's your name?"

The boy seemed satisfied enough with that reply. "My name is Francis. I'm looking for my dad. I thought I saw him walking down the road, but now he seems to be gone."

"We saw a man walk up to that house. Was that him?" Auggie knew the answer even as he asked. He knew that this was Francis Darwin, Charles Darwin's son. Francis would grow up to be a famous scientist himself, but for now he was just a kid like Auggie.

"I bet he's heading to the Sandwalk for his afternoon stroll. I'm going to go find him. Want to come along?"

"Sure," Emily said as they began to follow. "But what's the Sandwalk?"

"Oh, it's just a path where he does his thinking." Francis led them through the garden toward a row of trees lining the sandy path. There, they found Charles Darwin walking slowly away from the garden. They hurried to catch him.

"Father, these are some new friends of mine. Emily and Auggie. They are out exploring while their parents are visiting the town."

"Well, hello there. Pleased to meet you. Won't you join me while I walk along my thinking path?" Mr. Darwin had a twinkle in his eye as he looked carefully at Auggie, clearly noticing the snow pants and parka that Auggie still wore.

"Love to," replied Emily as they followed along the path. "What is it that you're thinking about?"

"Great question, young lady. I'm just finishing up a book in which I propose a theory about the way plant and animal species change over time. I've based it on my many observations of plants and animals, but now there's a professor visiting me from a prestigious university in London and he is trying to convince me that I'm wrong.

He has showed me observations and plants and animals that conflict with my theory. He's renting the old blacksmith shop in town to use as a lab. I was just there and he showed me samples that just did not seem right to me, but he claims they disprove my theory. So now I'm not sure what to do. I'm trying to decide if I should go ahead and publish my book, anyway."

"Well, it sounds like you're pretty suspicious about what he's telling you," said Auggie in a voice that trembled with nervousness. "Do you think he's telling the truth?"

"Truth, you say? That's a very good question." Mr. Darwin came to a stop in the middle of the path. "So hard to tell truth from trickery these days, don't you think? I have encountered so many people that are devoted to trickery rather than the truth that I have trouble telling the difference myself, sometimes. Yes, indeed, truth versus trickery. So hard to tell one from the other, especially when the one using trickery is very good at it."

Something about the way Mr. Darwin said, "truth versus trickery," caught Auggie's attention. It was as if he was talking about a contest that had been going on for centuries, one that everyone knew about, one that he himself was involved in, and one that Auggie and Emily should know about.

Except that Auggie did not know about it.

The only time he had ever heard those two words used in the same sentence was when his father was explaining one of his books to Auggie. It was one of those dusty old philosophy books, written centuries earlier in ancient Greece, and Auggie's father was using it to make some point or another.

Auggie didn't remember what the point was because he hadn't really been paying attention at the time. That was usually the way it worked: his dad would start explaining something and Auggie would pay attention for a sentence or two before his mind drifted to something else.

Now, he wished he had paid attention. Whatever his dad may have been trying to explain to him might be useful to know at this point.

"Oh, well," Mr. Darwin sighed. "The battle between truth and trickery isn't going to end today, if it ever ends at all. Let's keep moving."

Just then, Emily stopped and bent over as if to tie her shoe. "Go ahead. We'll catch up."

As Charles and Francis Darwin walked ahead, Emily whispered to Auggie. "That must be what Mr. Coyote is up to. He's trying to get Mr. Darwin not to publish the book. That must be why we're here. I just wish I had paid more attention in class, because I'm not sure if that book is *supposed* to be published."

Auggie did not hesitate. "Absolutely it is supposed to be published. That is a very important book, and the theory of natural selection that he proposes is the basis of all modern natural science. Most of the things we know about plants and animals started with Mr. Darwin's theory. I don't know what Mr. Coyote showed him, but I'm pretty sure he was trying to trick him."

"Okay, I'm not sure why the Time Vultures want to change this part of history, but they must have a reason. And I guess it's not really our job to know why. We just need to make sure they don't succeed."

They walked briskly to catch up with the Darwins. Emily was the first to speak. "You know, Mr. Darwin, I don't know this professor you mentioned. What I do know is this: I only trust the things I can verify, the facts I can check for myself. So if you can't verify his data, I'd be skeptical. Also, if you've spent years developing this theory and it fits with all the observations you've made, and you're sure that your own data are accurate, I think you should go ahead and publish your book."

"That's true," Auggie said. "Even if you've made a few mistakes, other scientists will eventually figure that out. But if you're right, and you don't publish it, wouldn't that be a greater loss?"

"You know, you kids make good sense. I just wish I had your confidence." Mr. Darwin shook his head as he walked.

Francis had been quiet for a long time, but now he chimed in with a question that to Auggie seemed totally out of place: "Hey Emily, do you know the secret to wisdom and happiness?"

Emily's head snapped around and looked at Francis and then she answered immediately, as if she had been waiting for this question all day: "The secret to wisdom is reflection. The secret to happiness is to be true to yourself." Then she turned to Auggie and winked.

Auggie was baffled. He felt like Francis and Emily were carrying on a conversation that he didn't understand. He thought Francis's question was out of place, but then Emily seemed to know exactly what he was asking, and acted as if there was nothing unusual in this question. Auggie wondered what they knew that he didn't.

"Yep, exactly, be true to yourself." Francis gave her a long look and then turned to his father. "Maybe you should try that, father."

Mr. Darwin stopped as if frozen in his tracks, staring first at Francis then at Emily and then letting his eyes rest on Auggie. Auggie could see a hint of recognition in his eyes, as if Francis and Emily had reminded him of a conversation that he had had years before but had forgotten.

"Remind me again what your name is, young man," Mr. Darwin said with his eyes narrowed into a squint, as if he were trying very hard to focus on something behind Auggie's eyes.

"My name is Auggie, sir."

"No, no, what is your full name?"

"Augustine. Augustine Spinoza. Augustine Jeremy Spinoza." Auggie blushed as he stated his full name. He couldn't remember the last time anyone had asked for his full name, and he certainly couldn't remember the last time he had said it out loud himself. It was just too much of a mouthful, too many strange syllables all connected together, for him to say very often. And when he did say it, he always blushed. Every single time.

"Of course, of course. Augustine Jeremy Spinoza. I should have guessed it. So your parents call you Auggie, I take it? Very clever. Very clever, indeed." Mr. Darwin nodded his head in understanding, as if a great mystery had just been solved. Then he placed a hand on Auggie's shoulder and looked him directly in the eyes. "I've just had a wonderful idea: why don't the two of you join Francis and me in my study, where I can show you the manuscript I'm working on. It would be a great help to me."

Normally, Auggie would not have accepted an invitation to enter the house of someone he barely knew. His parents had been very clear on this matter: be very careful about strangers. But in this case, he was uncertain. On the one hand, he had only just met Mr. Darwin and even though Mr. Darwin was a famous scientist, Auggie really didn't know that much about what kind of person he was. On the other hand, he had a feeling deep inside his gut that it was important to convince Mr. Darwin to publish his manuscript, and he felt that as long as Emily was with him he was safe.

While Auggie was struggling with his decision, Emily did not hesitate one bit. "We'd love to help you out. I've always wanted to see what a scientist's study looks like."

It was as if she knew something that Auggie did not, something that made her confident that Mr. Darwin could be trusted.

So, just like that, into Charles Darwin's house they went: through the heavy oak door set against the plain white front of the building, past an entry parlor, up a flight of narrow wooden stairs that creaked with every step, down a narrow hallway and through the narrowest door Auggie had ever seen until finally, before Auggie had even thought about the significance of what they were doing, they were in a room no larger than his own bedroom.

This was Charles Darwin's study, the very room he used to do his research and write his books. At first glance, there was nothing all that unusual about the room, except for the clutter on the desk, the walls, and every available surface. Otherwise, it was a simple square room. The floor was covered with a mint green area rug with a floral pattern. Past the edges of the rug on either side stretched a wooden floor the color of root beer.

Auggie slowly looked around the room. At the center of the far wall was a fireplace surrounded by white marble and topped with a large gold framed mirror. To one side of the fireplace was a tiny nook with a washbasin and coat hooks. To the other side was a set of root beer colored wooden cabinets and drawers and bookshelves. The only light in the room streamed through a window to Auggie's right, past cranberry red curtains, giving the entire room a slightly dark and musty feel.

Against the wall to his left, Auggie could see a dark wooden cabinet with what looked like 100 drawers. Small drawers, no larger on their front than a pack of crayons, sort of like the drawers you would use to organize nuts and bolts or even Legos.

Hanging above the cabinet were two maps, one framed in gold the other in black. But it wasn't the maps that caught Auggie's attention. He had seen maps before. In the library, in the classroom, even in his own bedroom.

No, what caught his attention in this case was something entirely different than a map. It was a skull. Two skulls, in fact. Auggie wasn't exactly sure what kind of skulls they were, but they were definitely skulls. White, shiny, hard skulls. They sat atop the dark wooden cabinet like museum pieces. One of them was almost the shape of a human skull but with a chin and jaw that jutted forward, the other looked to Auggie like the skull of a bird because it jutted forward into a point, giving the appearance of having a foot-long beak.

They made for a startling sight, to be sure, but Auggie was so fascinated by the rest of the room that he didn't even give them a second thought. They had no more effect on him than the plastic skeletons and skulls the people in his neighborhood used at Halloween to scare young children. Auggie had never been scared of those things, and he wasn't scared now.

Undeterred by the sight of the skulls, Auggie kept looking around. Reflected in the mirror on the far wall he could see behind him an entire wall of books, shelved upon a wooden bookcase and protected by glass and wood cabinet doors. Of all the things in the room, this looked the most orderly, as if Mr. Darwin had taken great care to line up the books in a particular order, and keep them organized.

As Auggie's gaze settled on a large wooden desk at the center of the room, cluttered with papers, instruments of some sort, glass jars, and what looked like fossils, Mr. Darwin motioned him toward a black armchair that sat to the right of the fireplace, just in front of the desk. Emily perched on a wooden stool next to him.

Mr. Darwin sat behind a desk, cleared his throat, shuffled some papers around in front of him, and prepared to explain his theory as Auggie leaned forward expectantly. He had studied Mr. Darwin's theory in school, and he was pretty confident he could have explained it himself, even to Mr. Darwin. However, the way Mr. Darwin started took Auggie completely by surprise:

"Pigeons. Pigeons were the key. If it hadn't been for the pigeons I never would have figured it out."

"Pigeons? What do you mean pigeons? What do pigeons have to do with anything?" Auggie blurted out. He was flabbergasted. He had expected to hear about the Galapagos Islands, about natural selection, about evolution, about how species of plants and animals change over time. Not about pigeons.

"Well, it could have been many different things, but for me the key to developing my theory was pigeons. Not just pigeons, really, but some of the rather crazy pigeon breeders that I know. I don't know if you know the type: those who spend all their time trying to figure out how to breed a pigeon that can fly the farthest, or has the longest wingspan, the whitest coat of feathers, or even the narrowest of beaks. They are fanatics about the peculiar characteristics of their pigeons."

"Okay, but what does that have to do with nat—I

[44]

mean, with your theory?" Auggie froze for a moment after he spoke. He knew that he might have blown everything. Mr. Darwin had said nothing about natural selection. All he had told them was that he had a theory about the way species change over time.

Of course, Auggie knew what the name of the theory was. He had learned all about it in school. Unfortunately, that wouldn't happen for another 150 years. At this point in history, nobody was learning about natural selection or about Darwin, and if Mr. Darwin thought that Auggie already knew about the theory, he would be very suspicious indeed. He would surely start to wonder how a boy he had never met knew so much about a theory that he hadn't even published yet. Auggie didn't know what would come from this wondering, but he did know that if Mr. Darwin became suspicious of him his mission would be doomed.

Auggie waited expectantly for what seemed like an eternity, hoping that he had caught himself in time and that Mr. Darwin had not heard what he had nearly blurted out.

Fortunately, Mr. Darwin gave no sign that he was surprised or suspicious. Perhaps he hadn't heard, after all. Or perhaps he had chosen to ignore what he might have heard. Either way, Auggie felt an enormous sense of relief when Mr. Darwin continued talking.

"Well, one of the things I began to wonder as I traveled throughout the world, and even as I observed plants, insects, and animals in the natural world around my house, were the tremendous variety of characteristics within each species. Surely you have noticed this as well? No two birds are exactly the same, even if they are both of the same species. One might have smoother feathers or a longer beak or sharper talons than another."

[45]

Emily nodded excitedly. "Yes, I've noticed that. It's true of plants also, right? At least, it seems to be true in our garden and in the woods behind my house."

"Yes, quite so. Most would agree that this is true. What I have come to believe is something that not everyone would agree to. Based on my observations, I believe that the dominant features of a given species can change quite a bit over time, so much so that eventually an entirely new species can emerge."

"Wow, that sounds pretty controversial, but I still don't see what pigeons have to do with it," Auggie said in a confused but curious tone.

"Well, it is very clear what is happening when the pigeon fanatics breed pigeons to produce a certain characteristic. If they want to produce pigeons with white feathers, for example, they will choose from among the wide variety of colors of pigeons the ones with the whitest feathers and they will choose to breed those pigeons in the hope of producing offspring with white feathers. What happens in practice, though, is that only a few of the offspring may end up with white feathers, the others may be a light gray or even gray. So the pigeon breeders will repeat the process until, eventually, more and more of the offspring end up with white feathers. Not all of them, of course, but most of them."

"There will always be some variation among the offspring, but by repeating this process over and over, the pigeon breeders will end up with a larger and larger portion of white pigeons."

"And they could do that not just with feather color, but with any characteristic they wanted?" Emily inquired.

"Exactly so, and though they may not always be successful, what they are doing is consciously directing a change in the species to favor one characteristic over all others. It was this process that struck a chord in my brain as I was trying to understand how species in nature may change over time."

"But you don't think that someone is consciously breeding animals in nature, do you?" Auggie asked skeptically.

"No, no, of course not, my boy. I do think something similar is happening, but I don't think that anyone is directing it. What my theory of natural selection proposes is that the environment within which a species lives shapes the way it changes over time. Here's how I think it works: at any point in time, within a given species, there will always be slight variations. In the case of birds, for example, some might have longer beaks and some shorter beaks. Now, if the birds live in an environment that favors longer beaks—let's say, for example, on an island where the only food for birds is contained in large nuts that require a large, strong beak to crack open—you can easily imagine what will happen over time, can't you?"

"Well," Auggie said uncertainly, "it seems like the birds with the largest and strongest beaks will have a better chance of surviving and the birds with the smaller and weaker beaks will die more often. So, in terms of reproduction, there will be more of the birds with the larger and stronger beaks in each generation of birds. At least that's what it seems like."

"Exactly the way I see it, young man. Those with the features most suited to their environment will remain the strongest, will survive the longest, and will produce the most offspring. Over time, this will mean that a larger and larger portion the entire population of birds from generation to generation will develop beaks that are perfectly suited to crack the nuts on the island."

"So it really is just like the pigeon breeders," Emily nodded enthusiastically, "except that instead of a breeder deciding what features are best, the environment is selecting some features over others."

"Yes, and that is my theory in a nutshell, as it were." Mr. Darwin paused and chuckled at his own joke. Auggie had the feeling it wasn't the first time he had told it. "Species adapt to their environments over time. That is what I call the theory of evolution by means of natural selection."

"And do you have any proof that it is true?" challenged Auggie.

"Yes, I think I do. I could show you some observations I made. I have them here somewhere," Mr. Darwin said as he shuffled through the paperwork on his desk. "Yes, here they are. What you can see is th—"

"Father, time for dinner," said Francis as he entered the room, gasping for air. Auggie had not even noticed that Francis was not in the room with them. He wasn't sure when Francis had left, or what he had been doing, but from the way he was panting Auggie imagined he had been running up and down the stairs the entire time.

"Francis, my boy, why are you out of breath?"

"Oh, that is a very long story," said Francis mysteriously, "and I really don't have time to explain right now, as mother has asked me to make sure that you come to dinner immediately."

With that, they all proceeded down the stairway to the front door. Auggie felt an enormous sense of relief. It had been quite a treat to listen to Mr. Darwin explain his theory, but it also felt like a lot of pressure, the kind of pressure you feel when you're giving a presentation in front of the entire class or when you're taking a test that you didn't quite study enough for. But now the hard part was over, and there was nothing else to feel pressure about.

At least, that's what Auggie told himself as they walked slowly down the creaking stairway to the front door.

As he opened the front door to let Emily and Auggie out, Mr. Darwin rested his hand on Auggie's shoulder. "You know, children, you've been a great help to me. You've restored my confidence in my work, and I have no doubts now about publishing my manuscript. Can I impose on you for one more favor?"

Auggie and Emily blushed at the same time. The thought that Charles Darwin would need a favor from them was a little bit embarrassing. Even so, it took them only a second to reply in unison: "Sure!"

"Well," explained Mr. Darwin, "I need to get this manuscript to the post office in town, and that is a very long walk for someone my age. Perhaps you could come by in the morning and deliver it for me?"

"We would be honored. We'll come by first thing in the morning." Emily smiled as they turned to leave.

"Wait just a minute." Mr. Darwin held up his hand. "Let me show you the trees I've planted along the path up here. I'm especially proud of the third one from the end. It's very special. Can you see it there? The third one? The one with the carving in the trunk?"

Sure enough, Auggie and Emily could see it. It was a birch tree, covered with white bark except at eye level where the letter 'A' was carved in the trunk.

"That was one of my favorite specimens. Collected it on one of my most exciting journeys. I dug a hole right there about a foot deep before I planted it. Very special."

"That's nice." Auggie wasn't sure what else he was supposed to say.

Emily had a better response. "One foot, huh? That does look like a very special tree."

"Special indeed," Mr. Darwin nodded and winked again. "Francis and I have to get home for dinner. We'll see you two in the morning." They waved as they walked away.

Emily wasted no time. "All right, the first thing we have to do is find a place to hide until morning. If Mr. Coyote sees us, there'll be trouble. And then we should probably sleep. I'm too exhausted to think straight."

"Me, too," sighed Auggie.

"Oh, and by the way, Francis is a Time Watcher too. That stuff about being true to yourself is sort of our Time Watcher secret greeting. But did you notice how he disappeared when we were in Mr. Darwin's study? I wonder where he went."

"Yeah, and what was with the heavy breathing? Was he out running laps while we were in there listening to Mr. Darwin?"

Auggie and Emily spent that night sleeping on the cold, wet ground in the forest next to the sandwalk. They were both so tired that they took only the time needed to find a soft, sheltered spot beneath low hanging tree branches where they plopped down and immediately started sleeping.

No chatting.

No saying goodnight.

No lying awake waiting to sleep.

Only the exhausted sleep of two tired agents.

It wasn't until the next morning, when they both awoke to birds chirping and bright sunlight filtering through the trees, that Emily finished explaining what was going on. Or at least she started to.

The reason that the Time Vultures wanted everybody to sign an agreement to stop interfering in history, Emily told him, was sneaky and sinister: they wanted to gather the names of all the agents of the I.A.I.P.H. So they tricked everyone into signing the agreement by pretending that they were agreeing to leave history alone.

But they didn't intend to stop interfering in history at all.

"We call that the Grand Conspiracy," Emily said. "And it was a pretty clever trick. It came as quite a surprise to most of the agents that the Time Vultures were organized enough to get together and make such a sneaky plan."

"But why did they go to all that trouble? Why do they want the names of all the agents?"

Emily nodded her head vigorously. "Exactly. That's the key question. We know that from the start, they have been trying to make changes in history to gain power for themselves. But they never really seemed to have a clear plan. We always thought they weren't clever enough to figure out how to gain power from changing history. We were more worried that they would just mess things up. But at some point, something changed."

"Changed how?"

"Well, at some point they seemed to come up with a master plan of some sort. A plan that, if it was successful, would allow them to control the entire world. We're not sure how all the little changes they are trying to make in history fit into that master plan, but we know that we need to stop them."

"So the Great Battle Over Time and History is still going on?"

Emily nodded. "It's still going on, and it's much worse than before. It's not just that the Time Vultures are better organized, and that they have a master plan. That would be bad enough, but it's worse than that: one by one, agents have been disappearing."

That, Emily told him, must have been what the Grand Conspiracy was all about. The reason that the Time Vultures wanted a list of all the agents in the first place was because, one by one, they have been making agents disappear. They didn't kidnap them and they didn't kill them. No, what they did was make them disappear altogether, as if they had never been born. They eliminated them from the past and from the present, erasing them from history completely.

"But if they eliminated agents from history, how did anyone know they had disappeared? If they make it so that they never existed at all, wouldn't that mean that no one would remember them or, rather, that no one would have ever known them?"

Emily stared at him gravely and said in a low and almost sad voice, "so your parents really haven't talked with you about this, huh?"

Auggie shook his head. "Should they have?"

"Well, it's the reason they stopped being agents. It was pretty painful for them. I'm not sure I'm the one who should be telling you about it, but it does seem like something you need to know."

Now Auggie was curious and scared at the same time. He wanted to know, but from the tone of Emily's voice he felt like maybe he didn't want to know. Deep down, though, he knew this was one of those times when he needed to know the truth even if it might be a little bit painful.

"Please tell me. I would ask my parents, but they're not here. It has to be you who tells me."

"Okay, here it goes." Emily let out a long sigh. "You haven't ever met one set of your grandparents, right?"

Auggie thought for a moment. It was true that the only grandparents he knew were his father's parents, grandma and grandpa Spinoza. His mother's parents had died long before he was born, and so he had never met them. He wasn't sure what this had to do with anything so he replied with an almost irritated tone. "No, I couldn't very well meet them if they died before I was born, could I?"

"Well, no, I... Let me just say... Okay, I know... Boy, this is harder than I thought. Tell me this: have you ever seen videos of them? Pictures of them? Any letters written by them?"

Now Auggie was becoming annoyed. Why didn't she just tell him whatever secret she knew? Why did they have to trace his family tree before she told him what was going on? Did she always beat around the bush like this?

"Look, I don't know anything about my mother's parents. She never showed me pictures. She never showed me letters. And the few times that I asked her about it, she changed the subject so I dropped it. Why is this important?"

Emily had her hands on her cheeks now, as if struggling to figure out what to say, or else how to say whatever she was going to say without hurting Auggie's feelings. Then she stiffened and looked him straight in the eye. "This isn't fun for me either, you know, but here's the deal: one of your mother's parents used to be an agent. A pretty good one, in fact. But then one day, all of a sudden, it was as if both of her parents had never existed. They disappeared from history completely."

[53]

Auggie slowly shook his head. "That can't be. If that were true, my mother wouldn't exist. Plus, if they disappeared from history, how would anyone know?"

"That's just it. That's what's so sad. By the time the Time Vultures made your mother's parents disappear from history, your mother had already become an agent herself. The day they disappeared, she was on a mission in the past. Somehow that made her immune from disappearing. She returned only to find that her parents had never existed. Only her and the agent she was with, your father, remembered them. That's when the I.A.I.P.H. first realized that agents were disappearing, and unfortunately they have never been able to figure out how or why."

Auggie suddenly felt like crying. Not over the loss of grandparents that he had never known, although that was pretty sad when he thought about it, but instead from the realization that his mother had suffered such a horrendous loss and yet had felt the need to keep it hidden from him. Probably she thought that he was too young, that it would be too traumatic, that he would be scared that the same thing might happen to her.

If that's what she thought, then she was right. He *was* too young. It *was* traumatic. And he suddenly had a new and overwhelming fear that his parents and his sister would suffer the same fate as his mother's parents, and that he would be left entirely alone in the world.

"I know it's hard. Everyone says it was really hard on her, too. And on your father. That's why they retired when you were born: they didn't want the Time Vultures to have a reason to make them disappear. They thought if they stopped being agents they would be safe. Seems like it's worked so far."

It all made a certain amount of sense to Auggie, now.

That must be why his mother clammed up whenever he asked her about her parents, why she didn't have any pictures or home videos to show, why she had such trouble coming up with a birth certificate that time they went to get passports so they could travel to Athens. And of course it must be why his parents had told him nothing about Time Watchers and Time Vultures, or about the Great Battle Over Time and History. For them, it was serious business. They had experienced the painful consequences of the battle first hand. Surely, they must have had mixed feelings about him growing up to be an agent himself.

"But why did the Time Vultures want agents to disappear?" Auggie blurted out the question even as he struggled not to start crying. He could feel his lip quivering and his heart pounding. He felt his eyes watering and his throat tightening.

"We just don't know why they want agents to disappear, and why they want to make slight changes in history. Only the Time Vultures know. That's one of the things we're trying to figure out, but we haven't had much luck so far."

This sounded to Auggie like a hopeless battle. Traveling through time, trying to protect history, while all the while, one by one, agents were disappearing. Eventually, Auggie thought, there would be no one left to protect history.

It sounded to him like the I.A.I.P.H. was losing the battle.

Apparently, though, there was hope. Many of the great writers and scientists in history had themselves been Time Watchers. Some had even foreseen that something like this might happen. They also knew that there was a way to stop it.

[55]

All throughout history, these writers knew the secret of time travel and also the secret of how to stop the Time Vultures. But they didn't want any Time Vultures to find out that secret, so they hid clues in their writings and sometimes in their homes that would help future agents figure it out. Some of the clues were secret codes hidden in books and letters, others were actual objects hidden or buried. That's why agents spend so much time reading old books and letters. They're trying to figure out the secret to stopping the Time Vultures.

So far no one has been able to decipher all the clues and to figure out the secret. But for centuries Time Watchers have believed that a Time Watcher would eventually be born who would decipher all the clues and discover the secret to stopping the conspiracy.

"So we're really trying to do two things. On the one hand, we're trying to protect history from the Time Vultures. But on the other hand, were looking for clues that will help us figure out how to stop them once and for all."

"Okay, one more thing," asked Auggie, "why did Mr. Darwin make such a big deal out of my name? It was almost like he knew my name, like he had heard it before."

"Oh, yeah, well he sort of had heard it before. Not your name exactly, but the different parts of your name. You see, at some point Time Watchers started using the names of famous writers, philosophers, and scientists. It was sort of a sign of respect, but also a way for us to recognize each other. So in your case, Augustine was a famous philosopher and so was Baruch Spinoza. I'm sure I don't have to tell you about Jeremy Bentham, do I?"

"N-n-no," stammered Auggie, too embarrassed to admit that he hadn't heard of any of those people, let alone read anything that they had written. Almost entirely to change the subject, he asked Emily the only question he could think of, but one that seemed pretty obvious: "But if all of us are named after famous writers and philosophers, doesn't that make it pretty easy for the Time Vultures to know who we are?"

"Ha, you would think so. It would certainly make sense to think so. But that's the really clever part about it. Time vultures don't read all that much. They really don't study history or philosophy or even science. Most of them are more afraid of the library than they are of spiders or snakes. So it works perfectly, because we all recognize the names but the Time Vultures don't."

Emily squinted her eyes against the morning sunlight and stood up. "We'd better get going so Mr. Darwin doesn't give up on us."

Chapter 4: The Chase

*Or, why you should pay attention
to the lessons your parents teach you*

It was as beautiful a day as Auggie had ever seen. The sky was bright blue, the sun a dazzling orange, and the fields all around them a perfect emerald green. They could hear the sound of birds chirping mixed with the lazy buzzing of bees. It was, in short, the kind of day people write songs about.

Unfortunately, Auggie and Emily had no time to write songs or even to appreciate the beauty of the day. They had a mission to complete. So, without admiring the beauty around them, they hurried along the sand path until they arrived at Mr. Darwin's garden. They could hear voices from the front of the house, and as they walked around to the front door they realized Mr. Darwin was standing on his front step talking to someone.

"Hello again, children," Mr. Darwin greeted them. "I'm glad you're here. This is the professor I was telling you about, Professor Thaddeus Bucksnoggle from the University of London. I finally convinced him of the truth of my theory, and he is so impressed that he has offered to take my book to the post office himself."

Mr. Darwin's words barely registered in Auggie's head, because the man he was introducing them to was Mr. Coyote himself. Auggie doubted that Mr. Coyote was really planning to deliver the package to the post office. More likely, thought Auggie, he was planning to deliver it to the town dump.

Emily must've been thinking the same thing. "Well, we'd love to walk to town with him. Maybe we can discuss the battle between truth and trickery on the way."

Mr. Coyote narrowed his eyes and began to shake his head but Mr. Darwin was nodding as he handed the package wrapped in plain brown paper to Mr. Coyote. "What a wonderful idea. Enjoy the walk."

Out of the corner of his eye, Auggie saw Francis whisper something in Emily's ear and hand her a folded up piece of paper. She quickly nodded and stuffed the paper in her pocket, and then they were off, trailing behind Mr. Coyote.

Auggie didn't know what Emily was thinking, but he knew that he was scared. Mr. Coyote still had not even looked at Auggie. If he had, he surely would have recognized him, and that prospect frightened Auggie. But Emily seemed to have a plan, so the three of them walked down the lane to the road and headed up the road to town.

Emily slowed for a moment and motioned for Auggie to join her. Just as they did, Mr. Coyote paused in the road, placed the package on the ground, and bent over to tie his shoe.

"Quick, give and go," Emily whispered as she shoved him toward Mr. Coyote.

Auggie knew just what she meant. He had spent years practicing exactly this play. With his father coaching his soccer team and his basketball team, he practiced this play almost every day. It was simple: pass the ball to a teammate and then go to the goal. Or, pass the ball to a teammate and go to the hoop. Even in different sports, the play was basically the same.

In this case, though, they were not playing a sport. This was much more serious. Even so, Auggie knew that the play would work. He jumped quickly toward the package, snatching it from the ground in front of Mr. Coyote. As Mr. Coyote reached out to grab him, Auggie tossed the package back to Emily and took two running steps toward town.

He saw Mr. Coyote running toward Emily to try to snatch the package and, just as he thought the package was going to land on the ground in front of Emily, he saw her plant her left foot, reach back with her right foot and swing her entire leg through, kicking the package as if she were a goalie drop-kicking a soccer ball.

The package sailed through the air and landed right in Auggie's arms as Mr. Coyote whirled around and sprinted toward him.

"Meet me at the special tree," he heard Emily yell as he ran toward town with Mr. Coyote chasing him.

Now, some kids are good at baseball; they can hit and throw and catch with ease. Other kids are good at the piano. Still others are good at art or drawing or gymnastics.

What Auggie was good at was running.

Everyone knew it. His parents knew it. His classmates knew it. Even the man at the running shop who helped him pick out new running shoes every few months knew it.

And now, Mr Coyote was about to know it, too.

Gripping the package tightly under his right arm, Auggie ran. At first, he wasn't sure he would be able to escape from Mr. Coyote. Snow boots, after all, do not make the best running shoes. As he struggled to run in the heavy boots Auggie kept looking over his left shoulder. Mr. Coyote was getting closer and closer. Soon, Mr. Coyote was almost close enough to grab the hood of Auggie's parka.

It was at that point that Auggie started to think about

home. He thought about how great it would be to crawl back into his own house and his own time with his own family. He thought about how much he missed his friends at school. And then he thought one last thing: *once I complete this mission, I am going home.*

The thought of home was all he needed.

As Mr. Coyote lunged to grab him from behind, Auggie swerved to the left, switched the package to his left arm, and ran like he had never run before. He felt the toes of his snow boots digging into the dirt road as his stride began to lengthen. Soon, he had left Mr. Coyote far behind and he was all alone on the road.

He ran past meadows on his left and forest on his right. He ran past cows grazing along the edge of a perfectly green pasture. He ran past a farmer bringing supplies home in an open bed wagon. He ran for what seemed like miles, all alone except for the clump-clomp sound of his snow boots on the dirt road and the huffing and puffing of his breath in the cool morning air.

He ran and ran and ran.

As he ran, he gradually began to relax. He knew that Mr. Coyote would not catch him now, at least not on foot. Not by running. Auggie was too fast and could run too well.

The realization that he was close to accomplishing his mission filled Auggie with a sense of accomplishment and pride. He considered all that he had been through and all that he had learned since the day before: about time travel, the Great Battle Over Time and History, the Time Vultures, and everything else. He had met Charles Darwin and Francis Darwin. He carried in his hands one of the most important books in the history of the natural sciences, a book that would lay the basis for many scientific discoveries yet to come.

And he was an agent. It was that thought most of all that excited Auggie. To think that the day before he had not even known about the Great Battle Over Time and History, the International Association for the Investigation and Preservation of History, or the fact that his parents had been famous agents was surprising enough. But to think that he was an agent himself, and soon to be an agent who had accomplished a successful mission, was close to shocking.

He considered all of this as he ran and gradually his pace began to slow. In the road ahead he could see a herd of roughly a dozen sheep. They were slowly crossing the road, from one pasture to another, along the edge of a wooded area which met the road abruptly.

With his lungs burning and his legs heavy, Auggie looked behind him down the long stretch of road that led toward Mr. Darwin's house. Mr. Coyote was nowhere to be seen. He slowed to a walk and paused for a moment along the edge of the road. This was a perfect time and a perfect place to rest. He watched as the sheep with their fluffy white fur the color of marshmallows slowly ambled across the road, bleating and stomping as they went.

He was completely relaxed now, confident that his mission would be successful and that he would soon return home triumphant and proud.

Those feelings did not last long.

Just as the last of the sheep exited the road for the pasture on the other side, and as he prepared himself for the short run into town, Auggie glanced back the way he had come, toward Mr. Darwin's house. It had been only moments since he last looked down the long stretch of road, and he expected to see the same thing he had seen before: nothing but an empty road.

What he actually saw was something entirely different.

The road was not empty at all. There was a single, lonely figure there, perhaps 20 or 30 feet away, and it was approaching Auggie at a rapid pace.

The shock of seeing something on the road left Auggie motionless, and it took him a moment to realize what he was seeing. When he finally realized what was in the road, Auggie was so surprised that for another moment he was frozen in place.

It was Mr. Coyote.

That much wasn't surprising. The surprising part was that Mr. Coyote wasn't running. And he wasn't walking. He was riding a bicycle. Not an old bicycle from the 19th century, but a full-fledged mountain bike from the 21st century, just like the ones Auggie had seen all the college students using.

Where Mr. Coyote had found the bicycle, Auggie didn't know. He must've brought it with him when he crawled through time. Maybe he stashed it in the woods near Mr. Darwin's house and ran to it when he realized that he could not catch Auggie on foot.

Wherever it came from, the bicycle made Mr. Coyote very fast. So fast, in fact, that by the time Auggie realized what was happening, Mr. Coyote had skidded to a stop right in front of him, hopped off the bicycle, and snatched the package from Auggie's hands.

"I'll be taking this, and you won't be seeing it again," Mr. Coyote barked as he shoved Auggie to the ground at the side of the road and climbed back onto his bicycle. "Not ever."

Auggie could feel all the pride and satisfaction drain from his body as it was replaced with tension and fear and a sense of defeat. If he let Mr. Coyote get away with the package, it could change all of history. Not only that, but it would mean that he had failed in his first and only mission as an agent. It would also mean that he would have to go back and face Emily and eventually his parents and explain that it was his fault the mission had failed.

He knew that he couldn't let that happen.

As Mr. Coyote turned his bike back toward Mr. Darwin's house and prepared to begin pedaling, Auggie saw an opportunity. He grabbed a long branch that lay at the side of the road and, just as Mr. Coyote rode past him, he reached out with the branch and poked it into the spokes of the front wheel of the bicycle.

What happened next was not a surprise to Auggie. His mom had once spent hours explaining to him what would happen if a stick got caught in the front wheel of a bicycle. It was a long explanation, involving something called an axis of rotation and something else called a transfer of force. But the point was pretty simple: if a stick got caught in the front wheel of your bicycle, it would not turn out well for you.

Despite the explanation, Auggie had never actually seen what would happen. So, even though he wasn't exactly surprised at the result, there was something new and fascinating in what he observed. The branch acted like a brake on the wheel, and as the wheel came to an immediate stop, the back of the bike raised up and flipped over the front wheel, throwing Mr. Coyote over the front handlebars to the ground and sending the package flying through the air where Auggie ran to catch it.

With the package back in his arms, Auggie turned and prepared to run toward town to deliver the package to the post office. The problem was, Mr. Coyote was standing in the middle of the road on the way to town. He held the branch in his right hand, and he didn't look happy. In fact, he looked angry. He raised the branch above his head and walked toward Auggie with a scowl on his face and a deep, low-pitched growl coming from between his snarling lips.

Perhaps if he had read the Agent Orientation Manual, Auggie would have been prepared for a battle with a Time Vulture. Maybe there was a chapter on combat strategy, or even just a few pages showing special battle moves. Auggie imagined that he may have even learned that he had some sort of special power, or else a special sort of weapon that was issued only to agents. At the very least, he might have learned something about the strengths and weaknesses of Time Vultures.

None of those possibilities mattered now because Auggie had not read his Agent Orientation Manual. He hadn't even opened the package it was wrapped in. So he was left with no specific knowledge or special training, no secret powers or special weapons, and no clues about the best way to defeat a Time Vulture.

Mr. Coyote didn't seem to be thinking about any of those things. He seemed to be thinking about how to get the package back from Auggie, and he didn't seem too concerned about the possibility that he might injure Auggie in the process. In fact, he seemed to welcome the possibility. He strode quickly toward Auggie and lunged as he swung the branch at Auggie's head with a ferocity that Auggie had never seen.

Auggie ducked as he felt the branch sweep over his head. He could feel the adrenaline rushing through his body as he rolled to his right at the same moment that Mr. Coyote swung the branch at him again, narrowly missing him and hitting the ground next to him instead. The branch made a loud thud as it hit the ground and sent a cloud of dust back into Mr. Coyote's face.

Mr. Coyote blinked and coughed and rubbed at his face to clear the dust from his eyes. "It's time you agents learn that you shouldn't mess with us. We're going to make the changes in history that we want to, and you're not going to be able to stop us. You'll find that out soon enough."

"I wouldn't be too sure about that if I were you," Auggie yelled with a steely determination as he jumped to his feet and ran toward the wooded area at the side of the road. He knew that if he could just get into the woods, he would be able to outrun Mr. Coyote and make his way to the post office in town.

But Mr. Coyote had other ideas. He jumped back onto his bike and rode into the woods after Auggie, holding the branch in his right hand so that he was prepared to strike at any moment.

Most bikes would be useless in a forest. But Mr. Coyote was riding a pretty sophisticated mountain bike, and he was pretty good at riding it. He jumped over branches and weaved to avoid trees and logs, he ducked as he rode to avoid low-hanging branches, and he hopped with both wheels in the air to avoid branches and holes on the ground.

Within only a few minutes, Mr. Coyote was just a few feet away from Auggie, separated from him only by a row of trees and some small bushes. He swung the branch as hard as he could, missing Auggie's head by only a few inches. Then he switched the branch from his right hand to his left and swung again, hitting the trunk of a tree just as Auggie ducked behind it.

Auggie was running as fast as he could, weaving among the trees and dodging the swinging branch over and over again as Mr. Coyote chased and swung, chased and swung, chased and swung. A few times, he tripped and fell and was within seconds of being caught but saved himself each time by rolling one way or the other toward the cover of thick, low-hanging branches.

It quickly became clear to Auggie that he could not outrun Mr. Coyote and his bicycle.

He would have to stop and fight.

For some people, maybe those who don't spend a lot of time thinking or using their brains, stopping and fighting might mean just turning around and meeting brute force with brute force. For other people, like those who do spend a lot of time thinking and using their brains, stopping and fighting means something entirely different: it means using your brain to make a plan, a plan that weighs your strengths and weaknesses and your opponent's strengths and weaknesses and then outlines a strategy that leads to victory.

Auggie was the second kind of person, the kind who thinks. He knew he couldn't battle Mr. Coyote while he was on that bike, and he knew he needed to do something to surprise him and knock him off balance.

He had just the right plan.

With Mr. Coyote now directly behind him and closing to within striking distance, Auggie leaped over a large fallen log and, instead of continuing to run, dropped to the ground and rolled quickly backward until he could feel his back resting directly against the log he had just leaped over. He reached along the ground with his right arm and felt his hand close around a stick the size of a baseball bat.

At that precise moment, he could see the front wheel of Mr. Coyote's bicycle in the air above him. In the same way that he had avoided every other log and fallen branch in the forest, Mr. Coyote had jumped over this log with both wheels in the air in a maneuver that Auggie and his friends always called a "bunny-hop."

It was the exact thing that Auggie had anticipated.

With a level of speed and precision that surprised even him, Auggie jabbed the stick through the spokes of the front wheel with his right hand, grabbed the other end of the stick with his left hand, and pulled as hard as he could toward the ground. He pulled so hard that it felt like his shoulders were coming out of their sockets, and the force of the bike against the stick pulled against his hands so hard he thought his fingers would come off.

Much to his surprise, though, instead of his shoulders coming out of their sockets and his fingers coming off, something altogether different happened: his plan worked.

The front wheel of Mr. Coyote's bicycle stopped abruptly as Auggie pulled it toward the ground. The rest of the bike didn't stop, though. It kept turning around the stationary front wheel. As it turned, the back wheel went from being behind the front wheel to above it to in front of it. In the process, Mr. Coyote went flying over the handlebars and landed with a loud thud on the ground about 15 feet from Auggie.

Mr. Coyote had fallen for the same trick two times in the course of only fifteen minutes.

Auggie stood up quickly and shook the pain from his arms as he gripped the stick tightly in his right hand. The bicycle lay on the ground in front of him. He stood over it for a moment and then jumped with both boots on the chain, breaking it into several pieces that scattered on the soft, mossy forest floor.

Then he turned toward Mr. Coyote. "I don't know who you are, but I'm pretty sure your name isn't Thaddeus

Bucksnoggle. And I'm very sure that you're no Professor. What are you here for? What are you trying to do?"

Mr. Coyote rose to his feet with a growl. His face was twisted into a sort of grimace, but with the same snarling lips and evil-looking eyes he had before. "That's not something you're ever going to find out. Not if I have anything to say about it. No kid of an agent is powerful enough to stop me. I don't care who his parents are."

Parents? Does he know about my parents? Auggie thought as he watched Mr. Coyote come toward him with his branch raised high in the air, prepared to swing.

There wasn't time to think much more than that. He saw Mr. Coyote's eyes widen and nostrils flare as he swung the branch at Auggie with a ferocious lunge.

This time, Auggie didn't duck. He planted his feet firmly on the ground, stood tall and swung his stick with all the strength in his body.

The two sticks met with a loud crack, like a sudden clap of thunder in the silent stillness of the forest. Auggie and Mr. Coyote paused for only a moment, both of them somewhat shocked by the force of the encounter. Then they continued to swing, each trying desperately to land a blow on the other's body but failing each and every time. Each swing was met with the other's branch or was avoided by ducking or lunging to the side.

Auggie slowly began to gain confidence as the battle continued. *I can do this*, he thought to himself, *I just need to stay alert and be patient.*

They were moving among trees and bushes and logs lying on the ground, swinging and ducking and lunging and jumping. Auggie held the package firmly under his left arm as he swung the stick with his right arm. Over and over and over again he swung and dodged, swung and lunged, swung and ducked.

There was no more talking. There didn't seem to be a point in talking. Mr. Coyote wasn't going to tell him anything useful, and Auggie certainly didn't have anything to say to Mr. Coyote. He had questions, of course, but he was pretty sure that Mr. Coyote was in no mood to answer his questions.

Soon, Auggie spotted an opportunity.

Mr. Coyote had backed him into a branch that stood about as high as Auggie's shoulders. As he continued blocking Mr. Coyote's blows with his stick, Auggie could feel himself backing into the branch. It was solid, and a pretty big branch, but he could also feel it bending as he backed against it. He slowly pressed backward into the branch, moving slowly inch by inch until he had bent the branch back by several feet and held its coiled energy firmly against his back.

He was concentrating so hard on pushing back the branch and holding it against his back that he was struggling to defend himself against Mr. Coyote's repeated blows. He could tell that Mr. Coyote mistakenly thought that his look of concentration was a look of fear, and that he assumed that the battle was nearly over.

He was right. The battle was going to end soon. But it was not going to end the way that he expected.

Auggie waited until Mr. Coyote cocked his stick high over his head as if to take one last powerful swing at Auggie. His eyes opened wide and his face was covered with the look of victory. The look did not last long, for Auggie pushed back against the branch with all his strength and then suddenly dropped flat to the ground.

Mr. Coyote stood frozen as the look of victory drained from his face. Auggie felt the rush of air as the branch whipped over his head. He looked up and saw it meet Mr. Coyote squarely in the stomach with such force that it sounded like all the air came out of his lungs with a sickening sort of wheezing sound. He was thrown back at least 15 feet and fell to the ground, moaning but otherwise motionless.

Auggie did not wait around to see if he was okay. He didn't really care if he was okay. What he cared about was getting the package he held in his left arm to the post office, going to find Emily, and getting back to his own time and his own place and his own family.

So once again, Auggie ran. He ran back through the forest toward the road to town, leaping over logs and avoiding branches and weaving through trees until finally he was standing on the road with a herd of sheep in the pasture in front of him, the road to Mr. Darwin's house stretching off to his left, and the road to town on his right.

Without even pausing, Auggie wheeled to his right and ran toward town. He wasn't sure how long it would take Mr. Coyote to recover from the blow of the branch, but he knew that if he ran fast enough there was no way that Mr. Coyote could catch him. At least, he couldn't catch him without that bike. Auggie had taken care of that: no bike can work well without a chain, and Mr. Coyote's chain was lying in pieces on the forest floor.

It took him less than 10 minutes to arrive in town and only a few minutes more to find his way to the post office. The postmaster gave him a careful look as Auggie walked up to the counter and handed him the package. "This is from Mr. Darwin. He asked me to make sure it ends up in the mail."

"Just in time, young man. The mail wagon is on its way out of town in a few minutes. I'll make sure this package is on it."

[71]

"Thanks," Auggie said as he left. "I'll let Mr. Darwin know."

Exhausted but relieved, Auggie stood in front of the post office for a few minutes and watched the mail wagon drive slowly down the dirt road out of town, in the opposite direction from Mr. Darwin's house. It was the same road that Auggie and Emily had walked down when they emerged from Mr. Coyote's lab in the old blacksmith shop only yesterday, and Auggie's eyes followed the mail wagon as it passed that very building.

He was anxious to get back to Emily, but as his eyes came to rest on the old blacksmith shop he knew he had one more thing to do: he had to destroy the cold machine.

He wasn't sure why he thought this was so important, or exactly how he would destroy it. He just knew that if it was something that the Time Vultures used, and something that they thought was important enough to cart through history, it was important enough for him to destroy.

Looking around in all directions and seeing no sign of Mr. Coyote, Auggie ran quickly across the dirt road toward the blacksmith shop. When he reached the door, he found a chain holding it shut, secured with a rusty old lock. He tugged as hard as he could on the door, trying to pull it open as far as he could. After about a minute of pulling, he had created a gap between the door and the doorframe just wide enough to squeeze through.

Once inside, Auggie did not spend time looking around or exploring. Instead, he walked directly across the room to the cold machine that he had seen the day before. It was still covered with a blanket, and as he lifted the blanket Auggie saw the same thing he had seen the day before: five shiny yellow cylinders, like oxygen tanks, each with one end of a rubber tube connected at the top. Each limp, rubbery tube traveled from the top of its oxygen tank to a black metal cylinder the size of a shoebox. A larger tube connected the other end of the black cylinder to something that looked like a fan, and there was a small dial connected to the fan.

In the dim light of the blacksmith shop, the whole contraption looked like a strange sort of mechanical octopus except that in this case the legs of the octopus were connected to things like oxygen tanks and the head of the octopus was hooked to some sort of fan that, as Auggie discovered when he put his hand in front of it, was blowing the coldest kind of air a person could imagine.

Auggie had imagined that this would be a simple operation: sneak into the blacksmith shop, destroy the cold machine, and return to Mr. Darwin's house. But when he was confronted with the challenge of destroying the cold machine permanently, Auggie was at a total loss. He had no idea what to do. He was perplexed, he was bewildered, and he was confused.

There were plenty of parts, to be sure, but none that he could destroy with the sort of finality and satisfaction he had brought to destroying Mr. Coyote's bicycle chain. The oxygen tanks seemed impossible to destroy with the tools that he had, plus it didn't seem safe to him to start banging away at a metal tank filled with who knows what. The rubber tubing would be easy to tear apart, but just as easy to replace. Auggie looked carefully at the contraption, trying to figure out how he could disable it permanently. He had no idea how it worked or how to make it stop working, and he had no time to figure it out.

So, without a clear plan in mind, he began destroying it as best he could. He tore the rubber tubing from the valve

[73]

on each cylinder and from the central manifold, he grabbed a rock from one of the shelves against the wall and began pounding it against the valve on each of the cylinders, and he tore the black metal cylinder from the fan and stomped on it as hard as he could.

It felt satisfying to pound and tear at the cold machine, to destroy something that the Time Vultures found useful. As he pounded and tore and stomped, Auggie slowly began to smile. It was the sort of smile a person gets near the end of a long race, or near the end of a long day's work, or even near the end of a test that has taken hours and hours, when there are only a few problems remaining and the end is in sight.

His sense of satisfaction—and the smile that came with it—did not last long.

Just as he was preparing to smash the dial on the fan with a rock that he clutched in his hand, he heard the metallic click of a key in the lock of the door and then the sickening squeak of the rusty hinges on the door. He barely had time to dive behind a table in the back corner of the room before the door swung open and the room was filled with light. Seconds later, Mr. Coyote strode through the open doorway, walked across the room, and stood staring at the wreckage of the cold machine.

Auggie could hear a low but unmistakable growl emanating from Mr. Coyote's throat. It was the sound of an evil and ferocious anger. Mr. Coyote looked all around the room as he narrowed his eyes into a suspicious squint and slowly clenched each hand into a tight fist.

At that moment, Auggie was aware of only two things: first of all, he was trapped; and second of all, Mr. Coyote was very, very angry.

The door at the other end of the room stood open, as if

beckoning Auggie toward freedom. But from Auggie's perspective, it might as well have been closed and locked, because he was sitting hunched in a corner and a very angry Mr. Coyote stood between him and the door.

"I know you are in here somewhere, and I'm going to find you. You're not going to see your family and your home again. Not ever."

That was enough to stir Auggie into action. He stood completely upright as a shocked Mr. Coyote turned to face him. Then he cocked his right arm back and threw the rock he was holding as hard as he could, directly at Mr. Coyote's chest. It landed with a thud and sent Mr. Coyote staggering backward.

The success of the solid throw with the rock, and the effect it had on Mr. Coyote, gave Auggie confidence. Unfortunately, there were no rocks left on the table nearest him. There were only fossils. Fossils of bones, most of them too small to do any damage.

Except, that is, for the skulls. There were dozens and dozens of skulls. Skulls the size of a baseball, some even as big as a soccer ball. There was no question in Auggie's mind that the skulls were big enough to do damage.

Auggie reached over and grasped one of the baseball-sized skulls in his right hand. It felt nothing like what he expected. Instead of the hard, shiny, rock-like surface he had expected to feel, it felt instead chalky and light and even somewhat soft.

He did not take the time to analyze why this might be so, because by now Mr. Coyote had recovered from Auggie's initial throw and was striding toward him. Auggie took the longest wind up he had ever taken in his life and threw as hard as he had ever thrown.

It was a perfect throw: hard and fast and straight as a

bullet toward Mr. Coyote's chest. Auggie thought for a moment, as the skull sliced through the musty air of the old blacksmith shop, that it had the potential to break one of Mr. Coyote ribs.

Unfortunately, perfect though the throw may have been, and as hard as one might expect a skull to be, Auggie's expectations crumbled in an instant. They crumbled just like the skull crumbled against Mr. Coyote's chest: like a giant ball of chalk shattering against the sidewalk, sending small shards of chalk everywhere and creating an instant cloud of powdery white.

Auggie was baffled. A skull should not shatter like that. At least, not a real skull. The only thing that would shatter like that would be the plaster molds that Auggie remembered making in summer camp.

And then it hit him: the skull wasn't real at all. The bones probably weren't real, either. They were fakes, made out of plaster. This was probably the "evidence" that Mr. Coyote used to try to persuade Mr. Darwin that his theories were false.

So it *was* trickery, after all, that Mr. Coyote was using to try to convince Mr. Darwin not to publish his theory.

Despite the pleasure he felt in uncovering Mr. Coyote's scheme, Auggie knew that this was not the time to celebrate. He may have uncovered Mr. Coyote's trickery, but he had also unleashed Mr. Coyote's anger. That would have been no problem, except that Mr. Coyote was standing less than 10 feet in front of him, snarling and emitting a low pitched growl.

As he looked around the room in desperation, Auggie's gaze rested on one of the fishing poles leaning against the wall. Suddenly, he had an idea. It came to him in a flash, the vivid memory of a game he would play with his parents in the backyard on long, summer evenings when he was just a small child. His father would grasp him by the ankles and swing him around and around, picking up speed with each revolution, until he could feel himself going so fast he felt like a human propeller. He could remember everything about it: the smell of the freshly mowed grass, the feeling of the humid but cooling air across his face, and, most especially, the occasional splat of a summer mosquito against his arms and face. He could even remember the staggering dizziness he felt when his father finally slowed down and placed him on the ground. That was why they took to calling the game, "Mr. Dizzy."

Auggie knew that this was no time for games, but he also knew that he didn't have a lot of options. He grabbed the narrow end of the fishing pole, and, just as Mr. Coyote had recovered and began walking toward him, Auggie held his arms straight out in front of him with the fishing pole extended and began to spin in place.

This must've been what his father felt like when he spun Auggie around in the backyard after a long summer day, except that instead of joy and happiness Auggie felt only a sense of fear and urgency.

As he twirled faster and faster, Auggie could hear the sound of the fishing pole slicing through the air like a whip. Soon, he was going as fast as he could, faster than his dad had ever gone. So fast, in fact, that to anyone watching he truly would have resembled the propeller of a helicopter. Except that unlike a propeller, Auggie was getting dizzy. Very dizzy. So dizzy, in fact, that if he had to spin for too much longer he knew that he would either fall over or barf. He might even do both.

Fortunately, he would not have to spin for too much longer. Mr. Coyote, who apparently did not understand the physics of a propeller, lunged toward him and right into the path of the thick and solid end of the fishing pole, which hit him directly in the stomach with a loud thump and sent him crumpling to the floor, stunned and immobile.

Everything would have been fine except for what happened next.

Maybe it happened because he was still dizzy from acting like a human propeller, or because he was in too much of a hurry to get through the door.

Or perhaps it happened because his legs were still feeling a little bit wobbly and uncoordinated from the long run he had just completed, or even because he was still wearing those snow boots and they made him a bit clumsier than normal.

There were a lot of possible reasons that could have explained what happened, but Auggie didn't spend a lot of time trying to figure out which reason was the most important.

Whatever the reason, instead of gliding smoothly and quickly through the wide open doorway as he raced to escape from Mr. Coyote's workshop, Auggie ran chest-first directly into the door frame.

It was not the sort of gentle brush or soft glance that leaves a person stumbling and surprised but otherwise okay. This was solid and direct contact against a solid and unmoving object, and it felt to Auggie like it knocked all of the air out of his lungs, leaving him stunned and gasping for breath. More importantly, it knocked him flat on his back in the doorway just as Mr. Coyote was rising to his feet to chase him.

Normally, Auggie would not have been worried. He knew he was faster than Mr. Coyote, and on most days he was quick enough to hop up off the ground and outrun almost anybody. But this wasn't a typical day, and Auggie wasn't feeling his usual self. He had already run miles and miles, battled Mr. Coyote in the forest, and turned himself into Mr. Dizzy the human propeller. The combination of all that, plus the fact that he had just run into a door frame, made Auggie feel groggy and slow.

Trying to ignore the way he felt, he staggered slowly to his feet as Mr. Coyote lunged toward him. Auggie had only seconds to stumble out the door and close it behind him, right into the path of the lunging Mr. Coyote. He could feel Mr. Coyote slam into the other side of it with a loud thud, followed by a growling grunt.

Auggie felt the quiet satisfaction of another small victory, but he knew that small victories meant very little. In fact, they meant absolutely nothing unless he managed to get away, get back to Emily, and find a way back home.

He staggered away from the blacksmith shop toward the bakery, trying as hard as he could to break into a run but unable to muster the coordination or the energy to do anything more than stumble and stagger.

Auggie knew that he had slowed Mr. Coyote only for a moment. With a quick glance over his shoulder, he saw Mr. Coyote emerging from the blacksmith shop and striding toward him, less than 20 feet away, looking enraged.

Once again, Auggie tried to get his legs to run. He tried picking them up as fast as he could. He tried lunging forward with his right leg then his left. He even tried talking to his legs, telling them that this was no time to let him down, that if they were ever going to pick a time to run this was the right time.

None of it worked. His legs were failing him. He could

[79]

stumble and stagger and slowly walk, but he couldn't run. He was too tired and too dazed.

Mr. Coyote was getting closer now and in only a few more steps would be close enough to grab Auggie. At that point, Auggie knew, it would all be over: his life as an agent, his chance of getting home, and probably his chance of ever seeing his family again. He had no idea what Mr. Coyote would do with him, but he knew it wouldn't be good.

Even as Mr. Coyote closed in on him, getting closer with every step, Auggie remembered something that his father always used to tell him: opportunity presents itself when we least expect it, so we need to keep our eyes open and be alert for it.

He wasn't sure why that particular bit of wisdom popped into his head at this exact moment. Of course, he was always remembering things that his mother and his father had told him: brush your teeth before bed, don't run with sharp objects, never eat raw cookie dough, i before e except after c, blah, blah, blah. Those things all made sense to him.

Every once in a while, though, he would remember something that his parents had told him that seemed completely out of place, not the least bit relevant, and even a bit mysterious. He usually ignored those things, and most of them he couldn't even remember if he tried.

Why he remembered this particular bit of advice, he wasn't sure. Maybe it was the way he remembered his father looking at him when he said it—all stern and serious, without smiling at all. Whatever the reason, he remembered it.

It was a good thing he did, because that's what saved him: being alert and watching for an opportunity.

He was staggering past the town bakery, at the exact same spot he and Emily had paused the day before to watch Mr. Coyote and Mr. Darwin as they chatted further up the street. Everything was the same, including the same large man in the red apron carrying enormous sacks of flour from a wagon into the bakery. He was quietly humming as he worked, and a faint cloud of flour surrounded him. The man had just bent over to pick up another sack of flour and hugged it in front of his chest as he turned to cross the wooden sidewalk and enter the bakery.

This was Auggie's opportunity, and he didn't waste it. With Mr. Coyote only an arm's length behind him, Auggie strode as quickly as he could across the man's path, brushing against his belly only slightly as he ducked underneath the sack of flour that the man held in front of him.

If Mr. Coyote had been paying attention, he would have waited for a moment before trying to tackle Auggie. He would have noticed the very large and seemingly very strong man crossing the sidewalk with a heavy sack of flour. He would have seen that Auggie did not leave him enough space on the sidewalk to chase or dive or tackle.

Apparently, though, Mr. Coyote was not the type of person to stop and consider a situation before acting. He never seemed to notice the small details in a situation that could make all the difference. He was impetuous.

So, Mr. Coyote didn't wait and he didn't notice any of those things.

Instead, he chose that precise moment to dive toward Auggie and try to tackle him. If there had been no one in between them, his choice might have been a good one. It would have ended the chase once and for all, and Auggie would have been caught without any chance of escape.

Unfortunately for Mr. Coyote, there *was* someone in between them. Someone much bigger and much stronger than Auggie. Someone carrying a giant sack of flour. As he flew through the air, Mr. Coyote's expression changed almost in slow motion from a triumphant and victorious expression to a look of trepidation and fear.

Even as he flew through the air, Mr. Coyote slowly realized what had happened: he had not stopped to think before he acted, and the result was not a good one. Instead of tackling Auggie, he tackled the baker instead, breaking the sack of flour open and covering himself and the baker and the entire sidewalk with the pure white of baker's flour, like snow against the brown dirt and weathered wood of the sidewalk.

Auggie supposed that on almost any other day and in almost any other situation the town baker was probably a very nice gentleman. After all, someone who was mean or grumpy or nasty probably would not choose to spend their time baking bread and pies and cookies. Nor would someone mean and grumpy be happily humming to himself as he carried heavy sacks of flour.

Of course, this was not any other day or any other situation. On this day and in this situation, all the baker knew was that a stranger who looked like a coyote had just tackled him for no apparent reason and had ruined a perfectly good sack of flour.

Auggie had to give Mr. Coyote credit: even after the shock of tackling the baker, in the midst of a cloud of flour, he was resourceful and quick enough to try to gather himself and try to run away.

But he wasn't quick enough.

As Mr. Coyote scrambled to get to his feet, the baker

reached out with a single hand, the biggest hand that Auggie had ever seen, and clutched Mr. Coyote's arm like a vice.

"What do you think you're doing? That was an expensive sack of flour, and my wife just washed this shirt. Do you want to explain to me what's going on?"

Mr. Coyote began to try to explain. "I... umm... Well... You see..."

Auggie didn't wait around to hear the rest. He had been fortunate to get this opportunity in the first place, and he wasn't going to waste it. He could feel the energy returning to his legs, and he no longer felt dizzy or unsteady. Instead, he felt like running. So that's what he did. He ran down the same road he had come into town on, still feeling like he was running away from Mr. Coyote but this time, at least, he was running toward Mr. Darwin's house and, he hoped, toward home.

As he ran, Auggie realized that he had barely had time to consider everything that had happened to him in the past day. But the long, lonely run back to Mr. Darwin's house gave him plenty of time to ponder his situation. It was mind-boggling to think about. The apparent fact that he had traveled through time would have been shocking enough by itself. Adding to that the realization that others, including his parents, had been traveling through time for centuries was like a double shock.

What made the whole thing a triple shock, though, was all the information Emily had told him about the Great Battle Over Time and History. All the stuff about Time Vultures, about the I.A.I.P.H., about agents, about his grandparents disappearing from history, and about the Grand Conspiracy: all of it was enough to make Auggie shudder.

He realized now that he had inherited an enormous responsibility, one that he wasn't at all sure he was prepared for. You would think that to be an agent, he should have been training for years. Taking classes, reading manuals, practicing battle moves. At the very least, you would think someone should have told him that he was going to be an agent.

Auggie resolved to confront his parents as soon as he returned home. Whatever their reason for not telling him that he was likely to be an agent, it clearly was time for them to help him train. At the very least, he needed to read a copy of the Agent Orientation Manual. But more than that, he needed them to share their wisdom with him. If they had been such remarkable agents, they must know something worth sharing with him that would help him be a successful agent also.

Of course, all of this presumed that Auggie would return home at some point. He hoped that he would, but he wasn't at all sure, and this chilling realization froze his thoughts for a considerable part of the run.

When he arrived back at Mr. Darwin's house, Auggie went directly to the thinking path and headed straight for the tree Mr. Darwin had pointed out to them the day before. He guessed that this must have been where Emily wanted him to meet her.

Sure enough, when he arrived at the tree Emily was sitting on the ground with her back resting against the trunk of the tree. Her eyes were squinting and her brow was wrinkled in deep thought as she looked carefully at a piece of paper. She did not even look up as he approached.

"What's that?" Auggie asked.

"It's a note that Francis gave to me right before we left. He said it has something to do with our mission. As soon as he realized we were Time Watchers, and that Mr. Coyote was a Time Vulture, he started to worry about it. He worried Mr. Coyote would somehow find it and steal it. Anyway, that's where he was when we were chatting with Mr. Darwin in the study: he rushed to his secret hiding place to get this note. That's why he was so out of breath. But he didn't get a chance to give it to us until this morning. I'm sure it's important, but I can't understand what it means."

Auggie leaned over and looked at what was written on the paper:

> *Roses are red, violets are blue*
> *My father always told me, to yourself be true.*
> *Reflect on what you think, reflect on what you do*
> *If you listen very carefully, you will hear a special clue:*
> *In the shade of a tree that has grown very big*
> *You will find a special object if only you dig.*
> *You will know where to dig and where to look*
> *If you take a stroll where father conceived his book.*
> *It must be said and it should be known,*
> *The object you will find is useless alone.*
> *You must find other clues to the mystery*
> *Scattered in fragments throughout our history.*
> *When you uncover them all, you will win the race,*
> *For together they form the key to a very special place.*
> *To uncover the name of the location you must find*
> *You must crack this code using only your mind:*
> *U I F   Q B S U I F O P O*

-Francis Ebsxjo

Auggie read through the poem two times but still did not understand it. He turned to Emily. "What does it mean?"

"I don't know. I think I've read it five times, and I still

can't make sense of this gibberish at the end. It's confusing. C-O-N-F-U-S-I-N-G." Emily spelled out the last word again, but Auggie was becoming so used to it that he didn't even notice.

"Let's ignore that for now and try to figure out the part that looks like it's at least written in English."

So Auggie and Emily read the poem aloud and it slowly began to make sense.

"That stuff about being true to yourself and reflecting on what you do is just part of the Time Watcher secret greeting. That's supposed to tell us that this message comes from another Time Watcher. I'm assuming it's Francis Darwin, but I don't know why he used this funny word as his last name." Emily pointed to the signature at the bottom of the page.

"I think that's the key to some sort of code. It will help us figure out what the very last line of the poem means. But I think we should do that later. It looks like we are supposed to dig for some sort of object, buried in the shade of a tree. I wonder which tree? And how do we know where to dig?"

And then it occurred to him: "You know, Mr. Darwin made such a big deal yesterday out of showing us this exact tree. And he went to the trouble of placing this mark on it. He must have had a reason. I bet the 'special specimen' he was talking about yesterday wasn't the tree at all. I bet it was this 'very special object' Francis is talking about."

"That must be it," said Emily as she looked up at him, "and Francis told us that this is the path Mr. Darwin did all this thinking on. This is the place where he 'conceived his book'."

"Yeah, and he even told us that he dug a hole one foot deep. That must be where the object is buried."

Without hesitating, they both bent over and began to dig. They dug with their bare hands, through grass and weeds. They dug through soft soil and hard clay. They dug until their fingers became sore.

They dug and dug and dug.

And then finally, the digging paid off. Auggie felt some sort of small pouch and as he dug around it, Emily was able to pull it out. It was about the size of a small purse. He watched as Emily wiped the mud off of the pouch and reached inside. "What is it?"

Emily held out her hand and showed him what looked like a rock.

"That just looks like a rock."

"But it's not. It's something special. Look what it was wrapped in." Emily held up a small leather pouch with Greek lettering etched into it. "And it's not just a rock. It's red, like a ruby. And it's been carved into some sort of shape. I think we should go ask Mr. Darwin what it is."

Auggie bent over to look, but before he could even focus they heard footsteps coming up the path.

It was Mr. Coyote. And he was coming toward them. He was panting and sweating and kind of stumbling. He was covered with a thin layer of white flour, and the sweat on his face made tiny rivers through the flour as it rolled down his face.

Emily jumped to her feet and shoved the rock into her pocket. "Let's go. We can't let him get us. We'll have to crack the code at the end of the poem some other time."

They ran into the woods that bordered the path, weaving through trees and leaping over logs. They dodged low-hanging branches and stumbled through underbrush. At one point, they even had to splash through a narrow stream that wound through the woods.

At first, as they ran as fast as their legs would carry them, they could hear Mr. Coyote panting and stomping behind them, crashing through the branches that they had ducked to avoid and crushing the leaves and underbrush as if he was on a mission to flatten every plant in the forest.

It went on like that for what seemed like forever, but was probably only five or six minutes: Emily and Auggie running and leaping, Mr. Coyote panting and stomping in pursuit.

The chase was every bit as scary as the last time Auggie had been pursued by Mr. Coyote, because the stakes were every bit as high. If Mr. Coyote caught them now, their mission would fail. Not only that, the note from Francis and the box of Mr. Darwin's would fall into the hands of the Time Vultures. Auggie didn't know the significance of either one of those items, but he did know that he couldn't let the Time Vultures get them.

So, despite his exhaustion and the fear to which he had become so accustomed, Auggie kept running and leaping and dodging, with Emily matching him stride for stride until soon they reached a small grassy clearing in the woods, bordered on all sides by tall trees. At the far edge of the clearing lay an enormous fallen tree, the length of a school bus and the width of an automobile tire.

"Quick, let's hide behind this log," panted Emily as she darted across the clearing and leaped over the log.

Auggie did not argue. Part of him felt like they should keep running, to put enough distance between themselves and Mr. Coyote that he would never find them. But the rest of him—most of him, in fact—said just the opposite: stop and rest. His lungs were burning, his legs were exhausted, and his heart continued to race. He needed a rest.

Without discussion, they ducked behind the log and waited. They waited for the crashing and stomping of Mr. Coyote's footsteps. They waited for the panting and wheezing of Mr. Coyote's breathing. They waited for the low, chilling sound of Mr. Coyote's growl. They waited for any sign and any sound of Mr. Coyote.

They waited and waited and waited.

Eventually, after what seemed like at least an hour of waiting, it became clear that Mr. Coyote was not going to find them. Either they had gone too far and too fast for Mr. Coyote to keep up with them, or he had taken a wrong turn at some point and was headed in the wrong direction. Either way, they were safe.

Auggie was exhausted and for some reason was still trying to catch his breath. The only thing he felt like doing was resting. But he knew this was his chance to get more answers from Emily. He wanted to know what was in the Agent Orientation Manual, what the best way to battle the Time Vultures was, how he would know when his next mission would occur. He even wanted to hear stories about some of Emily's missions. There was so much he wanted to know, and this seemed like the time to start asking questions.

But even as he was turning his gaze to Emily and organizing his thoughts so that he could start asking her questions, Auggie was a bit startled by what he saw: instead of resting or thinking or watching for Mr. Coyote, Emily was slowly and methodically tearing chunks of wood off of the rotten log.

"I can feel the tingling. I think this is my way home." Emily glanced at him as she tore chunks of wood off of the log, making a hole about two feet across. She stuck one arm into the hole as she looked at him. "Hey, thanks for helping me complete the mission. I hope we see each other again. Oh, by the way, where you live?"

"Cambridge. In Massachusetts," Auggie replied as he watched her arms, then her head, then her shoulders and torso, and finally her legs and feet disappear into the hole in the log. He wasn't sure she had even heard him. Curious, he reached his arm into the hole and was surprised to find that his hand soon bumped up against the inside of the log. Apparently, this was only a hole in time for Emily. For Auggie, it was just a hole in a log.

He sat there for at least another hour, feeling the sun soak his head and listening to the birds in the forest. He suddenly felt drowsy and so he slumped behind the log and lay down on the soft mossy floor of the forest. He felt the gentle breeze across his face and heard the soft rustling of the leaves on the trees. And then, without even realizing it, he was asleep.

Chapter 5: The Homecoming
*Or, why you should never
take for granted the world you live in*

Auggie awoke to the sharp crack of a breaking branch. He wasn't sure when he had fallen asleep or how long he had been sleeping, but now he was awake and alert in a frozen stillness. From across the clearing, he could hear footsteps and the occasional snapping of broken twigs. He slowly peered over the fallen log, looking in the direction of the noise.

On the other side of the clearing, he could see Mr. Coyote walking among the trees, looking slowly from side to side, squinting his eyes into narrow slits.

Auggie was startled and confused. Startled by the sight of Mr. Coyote. Confused about how Mr. Coyote had known where to look for him. Surely, it was not an accident that of all the places to look, Mr. Coyote had so quickly narrowed it down to the area where Auggie was hiding.

Auggie did not take the time to figure out how this could have been so. It was too important at this point just to escape, and so as he ducked behind the log and rested his head on the soft mossy forest floor, he focused all his energies on making an escape plan.

He knew just what he should do: to distract Mr. Coyote, he would grasp a rock with one hand and throw it as far as he could into the woods. Then, when Mr. Coyote was looking in the other direction, he would run as fast as he could back to Mr. Darwin's house. Once he arrived, he was

[91]

certain that Mr. Darwin would be able to protect him.

As he reached around on the forest floor for a suitable rock, Auggie could feel a quivering nervousness in his stomach and a tingling in his fingers and toes.

For a moment, he thought he was just scared.

Then he realized what was happening: he was near a hole in time.

He lifted his head again and looked at the forest floor. There, in the middle of a green blanket of moss, he could see a tiny black hole. It didn't look all that special, but it was a deep, dark, familiar shade of black. Auggie knew immediately what it was. He reached out with his right index finger and tore at the mossy edges of the hole until the hole was as big as his fist.

Slowly, he stuck his right hand into the hole. Sure enough, all he could feel was emptiness. No dirt. No roots. Nothing. Nothing but emptiness.

Auggie could hear the footsteps getting closer as he scrambled to tear away the moss. Even so, what struck him most of all at that moment was the intensity of the tingling. It was stronger, deeper, and sharper than before, almost as if there were someone controlling a tingling machine, and he had turned the intensity dial almost all the way up. Auggie could feel it in his fingers and in his toes, in his arms and his legs, on his scalp and his chin. Even his eardrums trembled at the intensity of the tingling.

Despite the nearly all-consuming tingling, though, Auggie continued to tear at the edges of the hole. It was nearly as big as a basketball by now; not big enough to crawl through, but nearly so. He continued tearing, even as he heard footsteps coming across the clearing toward him. He tore and tore and tore at the moss until it looked like the hole was big enough for him to squeeze through, though just barely.

He knew that Mr. Coyote was getting closer now; he was probably close enough to see him and to hear him. Almost close enough to grab him.

Auggie took a deep breath and crawled through the hole head first, wiggling to get his hips through. Despite the effort, he could feel an enormous sense of relief spread throughout his body. He had made it. Just seconds more and he would be through the hole and in the safety of his home. He thought about all the things he would ask his parents and all the things he would tell them about the mission he had just completed. For the first time in days, he felt relaxed and satisfied.

But the feeling of relaxation and satisfaction did not last long.

Just as he was almost through the hole, with only his legs remaining on the other side, Auggie felt a hand clutch his left boot. It was the worst feeling he could have imagined at that point. He had been so close to escaping that he had already begun planning the conversation he would have with his parents when he emerged on the other side, in his own home and his own time.

Those plans would have to wait. Mr. Coyote had found him, had a hold of him, and was pulling on his boot as hard as Auggie had ever felt anything being pulled before. Auggie's entire body felt tense and a wave of fear swept over him. He had been so close to escaping, and now Mr. Coyote had caught him. Unless he could escape from that grip, Auggie knew he was doomed.

Auggie struggled to escape. He tried to pull his legs through the hole. He wiggled to try to free himself. He kicked his other leg at Mr. Coyote's grip. He twisted and squirmed and shouted and screamed. None of it worked.

The grip that Mr. Coyote had on his left boot was too strong.

Knowing that he was in a horrible situation, Auggie tried desperately to think of a way to escape. He had tried kicking and he had tried squirming. He had tried twisting and he had tried wiggling. About the only thing he hadn't tried was rubbing a stick of butter on his boot to make it slippery, but that wasn't really an option. He didn't have any butter, and he didn't suppose that Mr. Coyote would let go of his leg for long enough to let him rub butter on his boot.

It was at that moment that one last option occurred to Auggie. It was an option he probably would never have considered, except that the very act that it required had been drilled into him since he was a toddler. Both his mother and his father had insisted, for as long as he could remember, that he take his shoes and boots off without loosening the laces one single bit. They would allow him to untie his shoes and boots *after* he had them off, sure, but never before.

It always seemed like a crazy requirement to Auggie. It was difficult and time-consuming and incredibly frustrating. And, after all, wasn't that the reason boots and shoes had laces in the first place?

Nevertheless, crazy as it seemed, Auggie had always followed their rule, untying his shoes and boots only *after* he had successfully wiggled his feet free of them. Over the years, he had become quite good at performing the maneuver. Without exception, he could wiggle free of all his shoes and boots in a matter of seconds.

For the first time in his life, he was glad—extremely glad—that he possessed this skill, because he knew that it would be the thing that saved him. As a smile slowly began to appear on his face, Auggie quickly pulled his left foot out of his left boot and through the hole until at last, with a great feeling of relief, his entire body was home.

At least, he thought he was home.

Until, that is, he opened his eyes and looked around. He was sitting on a splintered wood floor in the entryway of a house that was the same basic shape as his house. But this was not the house he remembered. There was no furniture. There were no curtains. There were no pictures on the walls.

What's more, this house was a dilapidated mess. The plasterboard was filled with holes in some places and falling away from the walls in others. Instead of lights, there were holes in the ceiling with wires sticking out. Auggie could see that one of the windows was broken and another was covered with faded plywood. There were cobwebs and dust everywhere.

Auggie thought that this house looked just like the pictures that his parents had shown him of their house when they first bought it. At that point, their house had looked like a dilapidated mess, too. His parents spent years fixing it up until eventually it looked just like the house that he grew up in, the one he called home.

If he had looked more carefully, some things would have seemed familiar to him: the banister leading up the stairs, the trim around the hallway closet, even the mantle above the fireplace in the family room.

But Auggie did not take the time to look more carefully. He did not want to be in this house for one minute longer, so he slipped off his one remaining snow boot, rose to his feet and walked out the front door into a cool January morning.

As he crossed the front porch (a porch that looked very

much like an old and run-down version of his own) and walked down the front steps (front steps that wound in a semicircular fashion around the oak tree at the corner of the house, just as his own front steps did) Auggie turned and looked at the address on the house.

He saw it but he didn't believe it.

The address was the same as his own: 318 Trelawny Street.

He looked next door and there was Mr. Ruttulio trimming his roses. Mr. Ruttulio looked over at him but did not seem to recognize him. "Hey kid, you better get away from that house. It's been abandoned for years and isn't safe. I better not see you playing in there again. And you might want to go get some shoes on. Looks like you lost a boot, there."

Auggie was confused.

It was his address.

It was his neighbor.

This was clearly his house.

But it was not the same as the house he remembered.

It was not the same as the house he grew up in.

It was as if his parents had never bought the house and fixed it, as if the house that Auggie remembered spending his childhood in had never existed, as if the neighbor that he remembered so well had never met him.

It was as if none of it had ever happened.

Knowing he would not be able to figure anything out here, Auggie walked up the street in his stocking feet with only two questions on his mind: if this was his house and his parents weren't here, then where were they? And, how would he find them?

Thinking that perhaps he had returned to a time before he was even born, Auggie reached down and picked up a newspaper that lay in the driveway of one of the houses up the street. But the date on the newspaper confirmed what he had feared: he had returned exactly one day after his 10th birthday, on January the 25th, just as he should have.

What he saw next made his scalp tingle and his hair stand on end.

Normally, he might not have noticed it, but as his focus moved away from the date on the front page of the newspaper, it was attracted to something else: positioned in the center of the front page was a large picture of a familiar face underneath a headline that read, "President Bucksnoggle inaugurated President of the United States."

Auggie barely recognized the face at first amid the banners and balloons and people dressed up in suits. It may have even been a few seconds before the realization hit him with the force of a sledgehammer: the person in the photo, the one being inaugurated as President of the United States, was none other than Mr. Coyote.

What?! Auggie wasn't sure how this was possible. Surely there was some mistake. Perhaps he was dreaming. He pinched his arm, slapped his face, and pulled his hair, but nothing changed. He seemed to be wide awake, and the picture on the newspaper had not changed a bit.

Auggie did not have time to make sense of his situation because just as he set the newspaper back on the ground, the school bus stopped right in front of him and opened its doors.

Auggie got on the bus without even looking at the bus driver or the other kids. But he quickly noticed that everyone else seemed to be looking at him. He thought perhaps it was because he was wearing snow pants and a parka. Or maybe because all he had on his feet were snow socks.

But he soon discovered that it was something else: none of these kids recognized him.

Kids he had been riding the bus with and going to school with for years looked at him with the sort of fascination usually reserved for new kids. And when he sat in his usual seat next to Oliver, who he had been sitting next to every morning for three years, he was stunned by what Oliver said: "Hi, I'm Oliver. Did you just move here or something?"

"Uhhh...Yeah, I guess." Auggie wasn't sure what was going on, but he knew that he couldn't explain it. So he held out his hand and introduced himself to a boy who had been his friend since kindergarten but now didn't seem to recognize him. "I'm Auggie."

When he arrived at school, Auggie wanted to run straight to the computer in the library so he could check his e-mail. Perhaps his parents had left him a message. But he had only taken two steps off the bus when Mrs. Peppersnell grabbed him by the arm and pulled him toward the main office. "You look like you must be new. Let's go get you checked in. And maybe we can find some shoes for you in the lost and found."

If anyone had ever asked Auggie to list his least favorite teachers in the entire school, he would not have had to think for very long before answering. Mrs. Peppersnell was at the top of that list. In fact, she was the only teacher at his school that he would put on a list like that. What's funny is that she wasn't even a regular teacher at the school. She was a substitute, but for some reason she seemed to be there every day.

It was hard for Auggie to explain what, exactly, he

didn't like about her. It was a bunch of things, really. For one thing, she was just plain mean. She seemed to go out of her way to make students feel uncomfortable or to embarrass them even when they hadn't really done anything wrong. For another thing, she had a habit of grabbing students by the arm so tightly that it felt like one of those blood pressure cuffs at the doctor's office. Then there was the way she looked at him. She would always stare for a second, squint her eyelids, then open her eyes wide and roll her eyeballs toward the sky, as if he had just told her a whopper of a lie so ridiculous that she couldn't even think about believing it.

What was most noticeable about her, though, was her tongue. That's not something you could say about most people, because we usually don't notice other people's tongues. But Mrs. Peppersnell's tongue was hard to ignore because it rarely seemed to stay put in her mouth. Every time she spoke, her narrow snake-like tongue would stick out a few inches from between her lips. It was shocking to see, and not at all pleasant. And the effect it produced on her voice was almost impossible to describe, except to say that it was the most unique lisp Auggie had ever heard. Every word she said that contained an 's' produced the effect of a long drawn-out hiss, like every single 's' was actually five or six in a row.

So as he followed Mrs. Peppersnell to the main office, Auggie felt the clamp of her grip tight around his arm and watched her tongue stick out as she said in her snake-like lisp, "Sssssit right here in thisssss ssssspot."

Auggie spent what seemed like hours in the main office. He filled out forms. He tried on shoes. He met the principal, the same principal he had known for years but who now didn't recognize him. He was given bus schedules and cafeteria menus. He was issued a library card.

When he was finished filling out forms, he went on a tour of the school. He toured the gym, the same gym he had spent hundreds of hours playing basketball in. He walked through the playground, the same playground where he had learned to play wall ball. He climbed the stairs to the library, the same library he had looked forward to spending time in every day for the last five years. And he was introduced to the librarian, the same librarian who had always remembered his favorite books but who now seemed to know nothing about him.

It was all very depressing for Auggie. To think that relationships that had been so important to him had evaporated as if they had never existed, that he had no idea where his parents were or how to find them, and that, as far as he knew, he had not a friend remaining in the world.

The first chance he had, during the first recess of the day, Auggie sneaked into the computer lab on the third floor of the school to check his e-mail. Given how his day had gone, Auggie wasn't even sure that his e-mail account still existed or that his password would still work. But he was pleasantly surprised when he tried to log on to his e-mail: it existed, his password worked, and he had two new messages.

The first message was from his parents and had been sent very early in the morning on the day of his birthday. In fact, it looked like it must have been sent just a few hours after Auggie crawled through the hole in the curtain. His mom or dad must have been up extra early that morning checking email; they must not have known that he wasn't in his room sleeping.

[100]

He read the message slowly and carefully:

Dear Auggie,
Happy birthday. By now you've probably read
your orientation manual. We know it's a bit
boring in places, but it's very important. There is
one thing that isn't in the manual but that you
need to know: the key is Athen

The e-mail ended abruptly, as if the person typing it had
been interrupted. There wasn't even a period at the end of
the last sentence. And there was no "love you" or "best"
on the end of it, which was surprising because he had
never received an e-mail from his parents that didn't end
with one of those.

Auggie was still trying to figure out the meaning of the
first e-mail when he noticed who had sent him the second
e-mail: Emily Emerson. He rushed to read it:

Auggie—must talk immediately. Something bad
has happened. Everything has changed. E-mail
me ASAP. —M&M

Auggie was beginning to type a response when Mrs.
Peppersnell burst through the door. "I don't know how
thingsssss worked at your old sssschool, young man. But
at thisssss sssssschool we don't go ssssssneaking around
during recessssssss time. Let'sssss head to the office and
get thissssss ssssssorted out."

She turned off the computer and led Auggie out the
door, down the stairs, to the main office. There, she left
him in a small room with a single brown fabric sofa as she
went to get the school principal.

As she closed the door behind her, Auggie's gaze rested
on the middle sofa cushion. There, partially hidden in the

[101]

swirling brown pattern of the fabric, he could see a tiny but unmistakable hole, a dark black hole, a hole that in the past he would have ignored.

But Auggie had learned by now that such things should not be ignored.

That's when he felt the tingling.

It had been there when he first entered the room, but he hadn't noticed it because he was so disoriented and confused. His fingers and his toes were tingling. His arms and his legs were tingling. Even his ears and his nose were tingling. It was that same unmistakable electric tingling he had felt when he found the hole in the curtain and the hole in the moss.

Certain that this was another hole in time, and in a rush because he knew that the principal was probably on her way to see him at that very moment, Auggie stuck one finger into the hole and tore at the fabric. He tore with his right hand and with his left hand, quickly expanding the hole until it was the size of a watermelon.

That's when he heard the footsteps. They were right outside the door. He knew he had only seconds before the door swung open and the principal and Mrs. Peppersnell walked into the room.

So he did the only thing he could think to do: he stood up and locked the door.

Then he tore faster.

He tore and tore and tore.

He heard the principal trying to open the door, jiggling the door handle and calling out, "Open the door please." Then he heard the sound of her key sliding into the lock. Just as the door opened, Auggie tore off the last bit of fabric and dove headfirst into the hole in the sofa.

Auggie was so relieved to have escaped, and his heart

was beating so fast, that it took him a moment to realize that he was in a much different place. For one thing, it was not cold and it was not dark. It was hot and it was bright. For another thing, something sharp was poking him in the back. And just when he had become aware of those two things, he heard a voice.

"Hey, you're sitting on my foot. Would you mind getting off?"

"Emily, is that you?" Auggie looked around but his eyes had not yet adjusted to the bright light.

"Of course, it's me. I crawled through a hole right after I e-mailed you. Right there in the cafeteria curtain. Not sure how I'll ever explain that one to the other kids. But it's not like it matters, because everything was different anyway. Nobody at school knew me. And my dad was gone like he never existed."

Auggie was somehow relieved that he wasn't the only one that this was happening to. "I know. Everyone is treating me like the new kid. Not even my friends know me."

"Yeah, well it's even worse than that. Something happened while we were back in time. All the other agents disappeared. Even ex-agents. Like your parents and my dad. I think we're the only ones left. I called the I.A.I.P.H. headquarters but it's not even there anymore. It's a Starbucks now. Been there for years, they said. Y-E-A-R-S."

"But I got an e-mail from my parents. Doesn't that mean they're still around?"

"Not if they sent the e-mail before whatever happened that changed everything. I don't really understand why, but for some reason email can't be made to disappear from history. At least, not the email that agents send. Our software programmers figured out how to protect them."

"That doesn't make sense to me, but whatever you say," muttered Auggie.

"Yeah, I don't understand it, either. It's not important now, anyway. What's important is this: I think the Time Vultures must have succeeded with their plan. Seems like they've erased all the other Time Watchers from history. It must not have worked on us because we were traveling through time when it happened."

"But how could they have done that?"

Emily reached up to wipe a bead of perspiration from her brow. "I don't know. Maybe they went back and made sure that your grandmother never met your grandfather or that your great great grandmother never met your great great grandfather or something like that. Whatever they did, it's as if your parents and my dad, and all the other Time Watchers, for that matter, never existed."

Auggie hung his head. His brain began to fill with memories and images of his family, like a mental collage of experiences and events in his life. He thought about the first time his mom showed him how to plant carrots, first by digging a shallow trench and then scattering the seeds in the trench before covering it with a small layer of soil. And the first time his dad took him to a bookstore and showed him how to search for a book he was looking for on the bookstore's computer. There were other memories, too: trips to the beach, hikes in the mountains, learning to ride a bike, family dinners enjoyed on the patio on warm summer evenings.

As these thoughts flooded into his head, Auggie slowly began to realize that his own memories may be the only things left of his parents. That realization brought with it a sudden but deep sadness. He could feel his lips trembling and his stomach quivering and the tears welling up in his eyes.

He could also feel Emily looking at him.

He did not want her to see him cry, so he cleared his throat and asked in a quiet but steady voice, "So, what do we do now?"

"Well, I'm not really sure. I think we need to figure out the secret to stopping the Time Vultures' master plan. And then we just need to hope that once we figure it out we can reverse what has happened. Here's the thing: my Agent Orientation Manual has disappeared. They must have gone back in time and prevented it from being written, or something like that."

"What a bummer. I never even got to read it, and I sure could use an orientation," moaned Auggie.

"Well, I guess you are going to get an on-the-job orientation. As for the manual, it looks like instead of reading it for the first time you'll have to help me write a new one."

Emily was surprisingly matter-of-fact about the loss of the manual. Auggie wished he shared her calm demeanor, because from his perspective this was a major loss, and he was not all that confident in their ability to rewrite the orientation manual.

"Well, do you remember enough from the manual for us to rewrite it?" asked Auggie.

"I remember some of it. Most of it I think I just take for granted by now. But I'm pretty sure that between the two of us we can come up with something useful. Before we do, though, I guess we should get on with our mission. I think we need to start by figuring out the last part of that clue Francis left for us. It still looks like gibberish to me."

Emily pulled the folded piece of paper from her backpack. It still had smudges of dirt and mud on it from the digging they had done. They looked again at the last section:

> *To uncover the name of the location you must find*
> *You must crack this code using only your mind:*
> *U I F   Q B S U I F O P O*

> *-Francis Ebsxjo*

Auggie had not told Emily at the time, but even as they stood in the shade of Mr. Darwin's special tree he had known right away that this last line was not gibberish.

It was a code.

And he knew exactly how to crack it.

It wasn't that Francis had told him. And it wasn't that he had seen this exact code before. No, it was something else. It was because of the way he had spent his summer vacation.

Most kids he knew went to summer camps during summer vacation. Basketball camp. Rock climbing camp. Art camp. Nature camp. Even kayaking camp. Auggie had been to some of those camps in the past.

But not last summer. No, last summer he went to a camp that none of the kids he knew went to. In fact, it was a camp that none of the kids he knew had ever heard of: cryptography camp. That's right, cryptography camp. A camp for learning how to make and break all kinds of codes and puzzles. All day, every day, he learned how to crack codes: numerical codes, alphabetical codes, military codes, codes using Egyptian hieroglyphics, even musical codes.

Any code a person could imagine, from simple codes to complex codes, Auggie had learned how to crack. And as he looked at the code Francis had left for them, he knew right away that it was one he could decipher.

"It looks to me like Francis has left us a pretty simple key for solving this code. We know his last name is Darwin. But instead of using his last name, he has replaced it with '*Ebsxjo*'. That can't have been an accident. I think it's a simple substitution code. He has just substituted one letter of the alphabet for another. All we have to do is figure out the pattern of substitution."

"Okay," said Emily.

"Those codes can sometimes be very hard to crack. But in this case he has left us a key. All we have to do is line up 'Darwin' with '*Ebsxjo*', figure out what pattern of substitution he used for those letters, and then apply it to these letters on the last line of the poem."

Emily nodded as she pulled a pencil from her backpack and wrote the two words on the piece of paper, one on top of the other:

D a r w i n
E b s x j o

"Okay, so if D=E and A=B and R=S, and on and on, what is the pattern?" Emily looked at Auggie.

"I think it's pretty simple," said Auggie. "He has just replaced each letter with the one that follows it in the alphabet, right?"

Emily stared at the two words as her brow wrinkled. She looked as if she was figuring out a math problem as she slowly moved the pencil across each letter of the bottom word. "Yes, I think you're right. So then do we just use the same substitution pattern to figure out what the last line says?"

"Exactly," replied Auggie.

"Okay, so here's the last line." Emily pointed her pencil at the last line of the poem and the string of letters it contained:

UIF QBSUIFOPO

"All right, so T comes before U and H comes before I and E comes before F, so that first word must be THE."

Emily wrote out the letters on the paper one by one as they deciphered the entire line of the code. They both stared at the solution:

THE PARTHENON

"The Parthenon. So I guess that is the location that we need to find?" said Emily.

"Yep, I guess so. But I don't think that's where we are now."

The Parthenon was something Auggie knew something about. His family had taken a vacation to Greece two summers ago, and they had spent a week in Athens exploring the ruins of monuments and buildings from ancient times. He remembered spending an entire afternoon exploring the Parthenon, which to him seemed like a giant building made of endless columns. He remembered column after column after column. But he didn't remember much of anything else, except that on the day they visited the Parthenon, he did not eat much breakfast or lunch and so he was hungry the entire time.

Thinking about their trip to Athens suddenly reminded Auggie of the e-mail he received from his parents. That last sentence: *There is one thing that isn't in the manual but that you need to know: the key is Athen.* Did they mean "Athens"? Or did they mean something else? Perhaps something that started with the same five letters? What could it be?

Figuring out the answer to that would have to wait, because right now the most important thing was to figure out where they were.

Auggie knew that wherever they were, they weren't in the Parthenon. No, they were in the middle of a laurel bush. That's what was poking Auggie in the back: the stump of a branch about as big around as his arm. There were branches and leaves all around them, and he could hear the gentle, lazy buzzing of bees around the bush.

He shifted his position to look behind him, thinking that if he could find a way out of the middle of this bush, he and Emily could explore the area to figure out where they were.

But as he turned his head, what he saw made him freeze.

He was looking directly into the barrel of a gun, a long gun, a gun just like the muskets he had seen in the Revolutionary War Museum.

Except that those guns had not been pointed straight at him, and this one was.

His heart seemed to skip a beat as he heard a loud, gruff voice: "Whoever you are, you better come out of there very slowly. And I do mean slowly."

Chapter 6: The Governor

*Or, why paying attention
in history class is worthwhile*

Auggie barely moved. The shock of staring at a gun, one that was pointed right at him, seemed to have momentarily paralyzed him. He felt like he was frozen in place, unable to move his arms or his legs or even his face. He wanted to say something, but couldn't make words come out of his mouth. He had never been this frightened.

It was Emily that made the first move. She slowly put her hands up in the air as she tried to crawl slowly between the branches so that she could escape from the bush. "Take it easy, we're just a couple of kids. We don't mean any harm."

Hearing Emily's voice, and seeing the calm confidence she showed as she crawled carefully from beneath the branches of the bush, spurred Auggie into action. "I'm coming out, please stop pointing the gun at me," Auggie said sternly as he parted several of the branches with his arms and emerged from the bush with his arms raised in the air.

As they emerged from the bush together, Emily and Auggie found themselves on the edge of a dirt road standing before a group of about fifteen people and a dozen or so horses. It was a hot and humid summer day, and sweat dripped down the faces and covered the clothing of nearly all the people. A few of them were holding the reins of horses, and almost all of them were carrying muskets.

One look at the group of people and the clothing they wore told Auggie all he needed to know to figure out what period of time they were in. It may have taken a while for some kids, or even some adults, to figure it out. But Auggie grew up in New England, in Massachusetts, in Cambridge, right next to Boston, not too far from Lexington and Concord. And if there's one thing a kid growing up in Massachusetts learns it's what people wore in colonial times. There were always reenactments of the Revolutionary War going on in towns scattered throughout Massachusetts, there was a parade honoring the Minutemen, and there were even entire villages where people dressed up in colonial outfits to attract tourists.

Auggie knew even more than most kids about colonial times. It wasn't just that he had visited the museums, watched the parades, and participated in some of the reenactments. He had done more than that. At the urging of his parents, he had spent hours and hours and hours in every library and bookstore he could find doing nothing except reading about the colonial period and the Revolutionary War. He had even visited all of the archives in New England with his mother; she always claimed that she needed to visit them for work, but what ended up happening every single time is that her meetings were canceled and she and Auggie sat looking through letters and manuscripts and maps and drawings from colonial times. Maps used by General Washington's armies, letters written by Benjamin Franklin and Paul Revere, sketches of flags by Betsy Ross. All sorts of interesting things, and Auggie had studied them all.

It was clear to Auggie that these people were dressed in similar kinds of outfits, outfits that American colonists wore during the Revolutionary War era.

[111]

Even if Auggie hadn't been able to figure all that out, the first words out of the mouth of the man pointing a musket at him would have told him everything he needed to know.

"Looks like just a couple of kids, Governor Jefferson."

Governor Jefferson, thought Auggie, *as in Thomas Jefferson? The man who wrote the Declaration of Independence? The third President of the United States?* And then Auggie remembered: before he was President of the United States, before he was the Vice President of the United States, before he was Secretary of State of the United States, before there even *was* a United States of America, Thomas Jefferson was the Governor of Virginia.

A tall man stepped forward. He had long, wavy, reddish hair that cascaded down his head and was collected behind his neck in a sort of loose ponytail. His bushy red eyebrows sat atop deep hazel brown eyes which were themselves surrounded by deep wrinkles, like rivers collecting in a lake. The rest of his face was tan and weathered, like he spent most of his days outside.

"Sorry about that, children." Mr. Jefferson looked at them with an apologetic expression on his face. "You know, we're at war. The British have invaded Virginia, and we can't be too careful. If they capture me it will be a great victory for them, and I'll be executed for certain. I'm Thomas Jefferson, the Governor of Virginia. Well, I should say that I was the Governor of Virginia. My term as governor just ended last week, around the time of the British invasion. But that's a story for another day. What are your names?"

"I'm Emily. This is Auggie."

"Well, it's nice to meet you both." Mr. Jefferson held out his hand and gave each of them a friendly handshake.

[112]

"It's quite a frightening time for all of us, though. I believe in the War of Independence, but wars are never pleasant."

"That's for sure," Auggie said as he nodded. "But why are you out here on this road if you think the British might be here. Shouldn't you be trying to get away?"

"Good question, lad. We have been hiding at my plantation at Poplar Forest, but this messenger brought us news that the British have retreated and that it is safe to return to our home at Monticello." Mr. Jefferson turned and pointed to a woman standing next to one of the horses. Her face was partially covered by a bonnet that she wore over her head, but just as Auggie was about to look away he saw a bee fly into a small opening between the bonnet and her head.

So now the woman, quite literally, had a bee in her bonnet.

She jumped and spun and hopped and screamed. She twisted and turned and stomped. She tore at the bonnet frantically, struggling to untie the knot under her chin so that she could release the bee from this trap. Finally, she was able to slip her head out of the bonnet and flick the bee out of her hair.

Needless to say, it was a sight to see. But it was not as shocking as what Auggie saw next. As the woman turned her head toward him, Auggie recognized her immediately.

It was Mrs. Peppersnell.

That's right, it was the same Mrs. Peppersnell that was on Auggie's list of teachers he didn't like.

The same Mrs. Peppersnell that rolled her eyes whenever he spoke.

The same Mrs. Peppersnell that grabbed student's arms with a vice-like grip.

The same Mrs. Peppersnell whose tongue reminded

[113]

Auggie of a snake.

What she was doing here, Auggie didn't know. But he thought it unlikely that she was here to do something good. If his experience with Mr. Coyote had taught him anything, it was to trust his suspicions about people and to trust his own instincts. And what he suspected at this moment was pretty simple: Mrs. Peppersnell was a Time Vulture.

"Well, that was quite a show, Mrs. Peppersnell. Now that you are out of danger, let's ask these children what they think we should do." Mr. Jefferson turned to Auggie and Emily. "Mrs. Peppersnell tells me it is safe to return to Monticello. I was skeptical at first, but she eventually persuaded me. Not only that, she accused me of not being brave, and that made me want to return to Monticello even more. What do you think? Have you come from Charlottesville? Do you know if the British have left? Is it safe for us to return to our home at Monticello?"

"You know," said Emily, "we don't know much about what's going on. We spend most of our time playing. But my parents always told me I should be true to myself."

"Yeah," said Auggie, "and I've always heard you should not make hasty decisions. You know, the key to wisdom lies in reflection."

Mr. Jefferson's eyes widened just a bit as a look of relief and decisiveness washed over his face. He took a long look at Emily before turning to Auggie and gazing at him from head to toe before looking him straight in the eye and giving him a quick wink.

"Quite right, my young friends. You know, when we left Monticello a few weeks ago I was about to return to collect some valuable papers but fortunately I took the time to stop and look at Charlottesville through my

[114]

telescope. There were British troops all over. If I had returned to Monticello then, I surely would have been captured. So I agree: We should stop and reflect on this. No need to rush, is there Mrs. Peppersnell?"

Mrs. Peppersnell stood glaring at Auggie. She widened her eyelids and rolled her eyes. She was not happy, but there was little she could do. "Yesssssss, I sssssuppossssse that'ssssss for the bessssssst," she said in her slithery snake-like hiss.

"Very well, then, the children and I will hike to the top of that hill over there and gaze through my telescope to see if the way is clear. The rest of you will wait here for us." Mr. Jefferson pulled a telescope from a pouch on one of the horses and led Auggie and Emily across the road.

They walked across an open meadow dotted with violet and yellow wildflowers. Just Auggie and Emily and Thomas Jefferson, the writer of the Declaration of Independence, the third President of the United States of America, the founder of the University of Virginia.

Auggie wanted to pinch himself to make sure he wasn't dreaming, but his skin was still sore from the places where he had pinched himself earlier that day. Pinching probably wasn't necessary, anyway, because Auggie was quite sure that he was not dreaming.

Despite his excitement, as they walked Auggie's attention drifted to something else entirely. He was slowly beginning to realize that his parents had been preparing him for missions for his entire life. Sure, they kept the Great Battle Over Time and History a secret from him, and they had waited far too long as far as he was concerned to share the Agent Orientation Manual with him. For these things, he was confused and even a little bit upset.

[115]

But these emotions now receded into the background of his mind as he began to see that his parents had been exposing him to a program of training since the very day he was born. Cryptography camp. The give and go. The lesson about the dangers of putting a stick in the spokes of a bicycle. The advice about waiting for an opportunity. All that time spent studying colonial history and the Revolutionary War. These things taken individually could have been simple, run-of-the-mill parenting, the sort of thing all parents might teach their kids, and it may have been just a coincidence that they were essential to Auggie's successful first mission.

Beyond those seemingly innocent lessons, however, there was more telling evidence of a clearly designed training plan. First of all, there was the thing with the shoes. Auggie had heard many parents telling their kids to untie their shoes before taking them off, but he had never heard any parents except his own tell their kids to leave their shoes tied every time they slip them off. Surely there was a reason, and Auggie could think of no better reason than that this was a skill they knew he would need.

And then, of course, there was the emphasis that existed in his household for as long as he could remember on the simple act of peeling. Peeling oranges, peeling potatoes, peeling the shells off of eggs, peeling patches of old paint off of the house every summer and even peeling the bark off of the firewood before placing it in the wood stove.

Every act of peeling, from the mundane to the exotic, was granted a special sort of importance in the Spinoza household. It had to be done properly, it had to be done completely, and it had to be done with speed. But above all—and from Auggie's perspective the most important and annoying requirement—it had to be done by Auggie.

For as long as he could remember, he was the only one in his house who peeled anything. Everything that needed to be peeled was peeled by Auggie. He became so good at peeling things that he thought nothing of peeling oranges every morning to make orange juice and peeling firewood every evening so they could warm their house against the cold chill of the New England winter.

Peeling things had become second nature to him, so much so that he never even really thought about how good he was at it. Now that he thought about it, though, he knew that he was very good at it and that there was a reason the skill was so important. Without the skill to peel quickly and completely, he probably would not have escaped from Mr. Coyote back in Mr. Darwin's woods. Nor would he have been able to escape from school just as Mrs. Peppersnell and the Principal were opening the door.

It had never before occurred to Auggie that there was a good reason for all the lessons, the studying, and the seemingly nutty requirements that his parents had imposed upon him. He could see now, though, that they were making him into an agent even before he knew that he would become one himself. As far as he knew, this system of training was itself more important than the Agent Orientation Manual. It certainly had helped him succeed so far. Auggie wondered what else his parents had taught him that he would use in his missions. What else in his childhood that seemed so ordinary at the time would he come to realize was instead a lesson that would help him succeed in a mission crucial to the preservation of history itself?

He didn't know the answer to this question, and he really didn't have time to think about it for too much

[117]

longer. They reached the base of a tall hill and began to climb to the top, as Mr. Jefferson told them about the war, about how he didn't think he should continue being Governor of Virginia because he did not know how to fight a war. He told them how he struggled to write the Declaration of Independence, how strong his belief was in a government run by the people, and how much he looked forward to returning to Monticello so he could read and write and invent in peace.

Normally, Auggie would have spent a lot of time worrying about what Mr. Jefferson would think of him if he asked a question. He would have hesitated, thought and rethought about what he wanted to ask, tried to figure out what the smartest way to ask it was, and then, in the end, he would have chickened out and kept his mouth shut. But, for whatever reason, Auggie felt like he could talk without being self-conscious, and before he could even spend time thinking about it, he found himself asking a pretty straightforward question.

"Mr. Jefferson," he asked, "is independence really worth all that you're going through? Do you ever wish you *hadn't* declared independence?"

Emily stifled a small gasp and stared at Auggie with wide eyes, as if to say, "What sort of impertinent question is *that!?*"

But Mr. Jefferson did not seem bothered by the question. He rubbed his chin and thought for a moment, then explained, "It is an interesting question, young lad. Certainly I do not enjoy all that we are going through, and of course one would be foolish to enjoy war and all the suffering it brings. Nevertheless, all my travels and studies have convinced me that people are better off when they govern themselves and they become miserable when governed by far-off rulers who do not know them or share their interests. That is why I would say that independence is worth fighting for. Of course, it is not easy."

Emily nodded in agreement, and then quickly changed the topic. "So, you were telling us about your home?"

"Oh, yes, a wonderful place," replied Mr. Jefferson. "If we are able to return to Monticello I would greatly enjoy having both of you as my guests for dinner this evening. There are so many special plans I have that I would love to share with you. I'm designing the remodel myself, you know. Spent a lot of time thinking about details, but the most important thing about it will be the columns. I owe that idea to the Greeks. They're the ones that inspired me. The first time I saw a drawing of the Parthenon, I fell in love with those columns."

"Greeks?" Emily asked. "You know about the Greeks? Do you know how to read Greek writing?"

"Of course I do, young lady. I learned from the very best."

They paused about halfway up the hill to rest for a moment. Emily reached into her backpack and pulled out the pouch containing the red rock that they had dug up from beneath Mr. Darwin's tree. "If you know Greek, I wonder if you could help us figure out what this says."

Mr. Jefferson reached out for the pouch and looked at it very carefully. Then he looked up at Emily and at Auggie. "Where did you two get this? Not from around here, I'm certain of that."

"We found it with the help of a friend," replied Emily with a smile and a wink.

"Of course," Mr. Jefferson nodded. "That is enough for me. I can tell you what it says, but I can't tell you what it means. You'll have to figure that out for yourselves. The English translation is something like this: *Athena's smile is pure perfection, but the key to wisdom lies in reflection.*"

This was clearly a clue, but Auggie had no idea what it meant. He would have preferred a puzzle to solve, or a riddle, or a math problem. Instead, he and Emily were faced with a simple sentence that he had no idea what to do with.

Even if he had wanted to figure it out, Auggie did not have the time right now. Mr. Jefferson had already handed the pouch back to Emily and begun marching up the hill again. And his pace had increased, so that now Auggie and Emily almost needed to jog to keep up with his long strides.

Once they reached the top, Mr. Jefferson sat beneath a tall elm tree and held his telescope to his eye, peering across the fields and forests toward a house that to Auggie looked like just a speck in the distance.

"I should have known. There are British troops all around Monticello. If I had listened to that Mrs. Peppersnell, I surely would have been captured. I suspected she was engaged in trickery, but for some reason I didn't trust my instincts. Thank you, children. I would have liked to show you Monticello myself, but that clearly won't be possible now. Maybe I can tell you some things about it right here, and you can look through this telescope so that you can see it."

Mr. Jefferson spoke as Emily and Auggie took turns looking through the telescope. All they could see at first was a large but plain red brick house with white trim around the roof and windows. There were British soldiers walking in and out of the house, and wandering around the lawn in front of the house.

"It doesn't look like much right now, but I have big plans for it." Auggie could hear the pride in Mr. Jefferson's voice. "If you look off to the right, you'll see a small brick building. That's where it all started. We call that the south pavilion, and that's where we lived when the main house was being built. To me, that will always be the most special part of Monticello. And I do mean special."

Auggie wasn't sure what he should say. The building did not look all that special to him; it was small and square and built of brick with only one window that he could see. But Mr. Jefferson clearly thought it was special, so Auggie nodded enthusiastically and murmured "hmmmm".

Emily continued looking through the telescope as Mr. Jefferson told them about his plans for Monticello. He told them how he planned to connect the north and the south pavilions to the main house, how he planned to attach a neoclassical style portico to each side of the main house, and how he planned to place columns within each portico. He even told them about the weathervane he was planning for the roof of the main house.

He was about to tell them more when they heard footsteps coming up the hillside. Mr. Jefferson stood up and looked down the hill, where Mrs. Peppersnell was slowly but gradually making her way up the path to the top of the hill.

"She is persistent, I'll give her that." Mr. Jefferson shook his head. "I think it best that I tell her and the rest of my party that the two of you have gone home. It'll be fun to practice trickery on her. Turnabout is fair play, don't you think? Before you go home, though, you should really, and I mean really, think about visiting Monticello. You could go there right now."

"Won't that be dangerous?" asked Emily.

[121]

"Yes, there will be danger. You must not let the British capture you. But you should be safe as long as you are careful not to get caught. It will be worth your trouble, I assure you. Don't forget: be true to yourselves. Oh, and you must take this with you when you go."

Mr. Jefferson winked as he handed Auggie a rolled up piece of paper, grasped his telescope under one arm, and then turned and quickly walked away, heading down the hill to intercept Mrs. Peppersnell before she continued to the top of the hill. As he took her by the arm and led her down the hill, Auggie began unwrapping the scroll Mr. Jefferson had handed to him.

"You know, that Mrs. Peppersnell is a Time Vulture. She's been a teacher at my school for years, and I never really liked her," Auggie explained to Emily as they watched Mr. Jefferson lead Mrs. Peppersnell down the hill and into the meadow.

"Yeah, well you probably have some sort of sixth sense about that sort of thing. You probably can sense that there is something not quite right about those Time Vultures even if you're not sure why. But I wonder why the Time Vultures are still trying to make changes in the past?"

"Well, it must be that their plan is not complete yet."

"Either that, or they know that we're trying to figure out how to stop them and they think they can keep us from doing that. I guess that's good news. It means there might be hope for us. Like maybe if we figure out how to stop them, it will reverse what they've already done." Emily had a hopeful look on her face and a wide smile that made Auggie feel hopeful also. She nudged Auggie to open the scroll.

The paper was stiff as Auggie unwrapped it and laid it out on the ground. What they saw appeared at first to be a very familiar document:

IN CONGRESS, July 4, 1776.

The unanimous Declaration of the thirteen united States of America,

When Coure f hman events, it becomes necessary for one eople to dissole the poitical bad which have connecd them with another, and to assume among the owers of the earth, the separate and equal station to which the Laws of Nature and of Nature's God entitle them, a decent respect to the opinions of mankind requires that they should declare the causes which impel them to the separation.

We hold these truths to be self-evident, that all men are created equal, that they are endowed by their Creator with certain unalienable Rights, that among these are Life, Liberty and the pursuit of Happiness.

The document ended abruptly, but Auggie knew right away that it was the *Declaration of Independence*. He also knew that something was wrong: there were words and letters missing throughout the first sentence. He knew that no writer as accomplished as Mr. Jefferson would make mistakes like those, even if this was a first draft.

The mistakes must mean something.

They must be a code.

"There are a bunch of mistakes in here. I think the missing letters form a code of some sort." Auggie pointed to the mistakes. "Uh-oh, I think we're going to have to be able to spell to figure this one out."

Spelling was not Auggie's favorite subject in school. He loved to read, he was great at math, and he was probably the best social studies student in the whole school. But spelling? Not so much.

[123]

"Dude, I can spell. Spelling is my thing. T-H-I-N-G. If you can say it, I can spell it," Emily said with confidence.

"OK, well how about if I tell you what the *Declaration of Independence* is supposed to say, and you keep track of whatever letters or words are missing."

"Sounds good," said Emily and she pulled a pencil from her backpack.

"Here it goes. I'm pretty sure I remember it. It should read like this: *when in the course of human events, it becomes necessary for one people to dissolve the political bands—*"

"Okay, stop right there. Here's what's missing so far." Emily pointed to what she had written on the paper:

in the soupvlns

"*—which have connected them with another, and to assume among the powers of the earth, the separate and equal station to which the laws of nature—*" Auggie paused as he watched Emily scrawl the missing letters on her paper.

So far, they had the following letters:

in the soupvlnstep

"I think those are the only missing letters on the whole page," Auggie said as he browsed through the rest of the page. "Everything else looks pretty accurate to me."

"Okay, so what does it mean? I get the first two words, 'in the', but I don't get what that word jumble on the end means."

Auggie rubbed his head vigorously as he stared at the jumble of letters. What could *soupvlnstep* possibly mean? Then it hit him: Mr. Jefferson had been very emphatic about the importance of the south pavilion. Could *soupvln* really be *sou pvln*, as in an abbreviation for south pavilion? If it was, then the only remaining letters would form a simple word: *step*.

That was it!

Auggie grabbed a pencil from Emily and wrote out the code, adding spaces between the words and abbreviations:

in the sou pvln step

"That's how I think it is supposed to read. And the third and fourth words are abbreviations for south pavilion, so once we write out the entire phrase it will look like this," Auggie wrote out the phrase on Emily's paper:

In the south pavilion step

"The south pavilion step? Is that why he had us look through his telescope at the south pavilion? I wondered about that. It didn't seem so special to me when I looked at it, so he must have done that so that we would understand this clue." Emily waved her hand in front of her face to chase away a bee. "Well, I suppose that's why he told us we should visit Monticello: there's something hidden in the south pavilion step."

Auggie nodded as he stuffed the paper in his pocket. "Yep, that's what I was thinking, too. And it must be important or else he wouldn't have encouraged us to take the risk of getting caught by the British."

"All right, looks like we have a long walk ahead of us. We should probably get going."

So they set out toward Monticello, walking down a switchback trail that descended the steep side of the hill opposite the side they had come up. They walked across an open field covered with the bright white flowers of Queen Anne's lace and the deep green of wild grass. They walked down a dirt road that showed the imprints of horses' hooves and the ruts of wagon wheels. They walked through patches of forest covered with undergrowth.

They walked and walked and walked.

Occasionally, they could hear British soldiers on horseback riding down the roads and through the fields. Whenever they sounded near, Auggie and Emily would seek cover in the nearest bush until it seemed safe to emerge. Then, they would continue walking.

As day turned to evening and evening turned to dusk, Auggie and Emily arrived at the base of the hill upon which Monticello stood. There, on top of the hill, they could see the main house and the south pavilion.

But there was a problem. There were British soldiers everywhere: in front of the main house, on the roads leading up the hill to the house, and even, occasionally, in the fields surrounding the house.

"What do we do?" asked Auggie. "If we walk up the road or through the fields, they will surely see us."

"Yes, I think that's right. We'll have to wait till dark. Do you still have your headlamp? That might come in handy."

Auggie reached into the pocket of his parka, where he had stuffed his headlamp just a few days ago. It seemed like years ago to him. That was back when he knew nothing about Time Watchers or Time Vultures, about the Great Battle Over Time and History, about the possibility that history could be changed and his parents could disappear. But now his life had changed, and it had changed in ways he could never have imagined just a few days ago.

As they waited for dusk to turn to dark, Auggie and

Emily crouched beneath the cover of a giant laurel bush along the entrance road to Monticello. They were still and quiet. Every few minutes they could hear the footsteps of British soldiers passing by on the road.

They sat and waited as Emily told him about some of the other places she had traveled and the famous people she had met. She had met General Washington at Valley Forge. She had met Julius Caesar in ancient Rome. She had even met Albert Einstein.

Then she told him about their names. Their names were not chosen at random, she told him. They were named after some of the great philosophers and writers and inventors that their parents had met when they themselves traveled through time. So Augustine's parents must have met a famous philosopher named Augustine, and someone named Jeremy, and someone else named Spinoza.

Finally, it was dark. Most of the soldiers had disappeared from the road and were now gathered in small groups in front of the main house.

Slowly, quietly, and very carefully, Emily and Auggie emerged from the cover of the laurel bush and walked along the side of the road up the hill, toward the south pavilion. There was a full moon in the sky which bathed the entire hillside in an eerie white light, punctuated by moments of total darkness whenever a clump of scattered clouds rushed in front of the moon. Every few minutes, Emily and Auggie paused to reorient themselves and make sure there were no soldiers lurking in the bushes along the road.

And then, after a moment of darkness spent paused beneath a giant oak tree, Auggie and Emily found themselves standing right in front of the south pavilion just as the bright light of the moon emerged from the covering of clouds and illuminated a single wooden step beneath a simple front door.

"There it is," Emily said as she grabbed Auggie by the arm and led him toward the step.

Just at that moment, though, they heard laughter coming from inside the south pavilion and they could see the doorknob of the front door start to turn. They ducked behind the corner of the building just in time to see two British soldiers emerge from the front door.

One of the soldiers walked directly toward the main house, but the other one lingered on the front step. His back was turned to Auggie and Emily, but they could see him peer up at the wall of the south pavilion, turn his head to look down the road—the very same road Auggie and Emily had walked up less than five minutes ago—and then gradually turn to face the very corner of the building where Auggie and Emily were hiding.

Now, it was frightening enough for Auggie and Emily to contemplate being caught by a British soldier. Surely, that would not have been a happy experience. The British were probably nice enough if you were their friends, and of course in Auggie's time the Americans and the British were very good friends. But at this point in time, they were at war. And one never wants to be captured by an enemy in a war.

That's what Auggie was thinking as the soldier turned toward them. But as the moonlight illuminated the British soldier's face, a flood of new thoughts and fears filled his mind. For there before him, dressed as a British soldier and standing on the very step that contained some sort of clue that Auggie and Emily needed to recover, was someone he recognized very well.

It was not a famous British general that he had read

[128]

about in his history books, and it most certainly was not a famous writer or scientist or inventor. No, standing there on the step was the last person Auggie wanted to see: Mr. Coyote.

Auggie felt Emily clutch his arm and squeeze just as he heard her muffled gasp. She had seen Mr. Coyote, too. Auggie could feel his heart beating faster as he held his breath and hoped that Mr. Coyote would not walk in their direction.

A gentle breeze blew across the hillside, carrying with it the scent of lilac. The clouds moved in front of the moon as Auggie and Emily waited. They waited as Mr. Coyote stomped mud from his boots. They waited as he stared up at the moon with his eyes closed. They waited as he looked around, squinting as if hoping to see something in the darkness.

They waited and waited and waited.

Just as Auggie had feared, Mr. Coyote began walking toward the corner of the south pavilion, the very corner where they were hiding. He took slow step after slow step after slow step until he was only steps away from the corner. Two more steps and he would not only see them, he would be close enough to grab them.

Then he froze. There was no sound, and there was nothing on the road or in the fields or in the bushes. But Mr. Coyote froze as if someone had called his name. He stood there, only steps away from Auggie and Emily, in a stance of stillness like a statue. And then suddenly, for no apparent reason, he turned around and began running down the road away from the south pavilion.

It took a moment for Auggie to realize what had happened. He had been preparing himself to be captured, to endure whatever kind of punishment Mr. Coyote was likely to inflict. But now Mr. Coyote was gone. Where he had gone, and why he had left in such a hurry, Auggie did not know. But he knew they had to move fast, because wherever Mr. Coyote had gone, he would probably be back.

The moon was behind a wall of clouds now, and the front step of the south pavilion was surrounded by a dim darkness. Auggie pulled his headlamp from the pocket of his parka, slipped it on his head, and turned on the light. "Come on, we have to work fast."

As they approached the front step, they could hear activity inside the south pavilion. They knew that if someone opened the front door, they would be caught.

Wasting no time, Auggie put his hands around the edge of the wooden step and pulled. He pulled harder than he had ever pulled before. Harder than his dad pulled to start the lawnmower. Harder than his mom pulled when she pulled turnips from the ground. Harder than he had ever imagined he could pull.

And it worked.

With a creaking and a cracking sound, the step came free. In the space beneath the step, Auggie and Emily could see a small container, about the size of a 64 pack of crayons. But this was no box of crayons. Even in the moonlight, it sparkled like a piece of gold. There was writing of some sort etched into its metallic lid, and a small clasp held it shut.

Just as Auggie felt his hands close around the cool metal of the container, they heard footsteps. Not soft footsteps, but the hard, loud footsteps of someone running. They were getting louder and louder, closer and closer, more frightening and more frightening.

Emily reached up and switched off Auggie's headlamp

as she pulled him away from the south pavilion to the shelter of a lilac bush. There, they watched as Mr. Coyote and a group of three British soldiers came running around the corner of the south pavilion and headed for the front step. They stopped before they reached the step and stood staring at it, lying there on the ground, detached from the stairway leading up to the front door.

Mr. Coyote looked all around and then began giving orders. Auggie couldn't hear what he was saying to the soldiers, but it soon became clear that he was telling them to search the area. They began to spread out, poking their muskets into the bushes surrounding the south pavilion.

It would be only minutes until they started poking at the lilac bush where Emily and Auggie were hiding. Auggie sat grasping the metal container, wondering what was inside, but knowing that this was not the place or the time to find out.

He was trying to decide what they should do when he saw Emily digging away the weeds and moss next to the trunk of the lilac bush. "Time for me to go. I can't pass up this chance, otherwise I might be stuck here. Good luck."

The hole was not yet big enough for Emily to fit through when Auggie saw one of the soldiers walking toward their bush. He knew that if he did nothing, Emily would not have time to escape through the hole before the soldier found them. So he did the only thing he could think of: he ran.

He did not run quietly or softly, the way a person might if they were trying not to be detected. No, he did the opposite: he waved his arms in the air, yelled and whooped and hollered, and stomped and spun around before taking off as fast as he could down the road, away from the south pavilion, away from Monticello, away from the lilac bush, and away from Emily.

As he ran down the road looking over his shoulder, he hoped the British soldiers would stop looking in the bushes and follow him instead. It did not take long for him to see that his plan had worked. All the British soldiers held still for a moment, shocked into a frozen silence by the sight of a young boy in a parka and snow pants waving his arms and making a commotion before running away.

Once they reacted, though, they all did the same thing: they chased him. They chased him down the road and through the fields. They chased him through the woods and over the hills. They chased him through creeks and meadows. They chased and chased and chased until eventually, as they panted and huffed and stumbled, they could chase him no more.

He had run too far and too fast for Mr. Coyote and the British soldiers to catch him.

Auggie slowed to a walk and paused to rest in a small wooded area at the edge of a winding dirt road. He could hear birds chirping and bees buzzing and somewhere in the distance the gentle gurgling sound of a stream or creek. He was anxious to examine the container they had found beneath the step of the south pavilion, so he wandered around until he found a small bush where he could hide and turn on his headlamp.

Once he sat in the shelter of the bush, though, he was overcome with an overwhelming feeling of fatigue. It made sense, he supposed, that his body would be tired. After all, he had hiked several miles to get to Monticello with Emily, and had run at least that far to escape from the British soldiers.

He closed his eyes, planning to rest for just a moment. But when he awoke, he felt the cool chill and bright sunshine of a summer morning. He had slept through the night. At first, he assumed the sunlight was what woke him up. Until, that is, he heard the stomping.

It was not a gentle stomping, but the loud and insistent stomping of something big. He peeked out from beneath the bush and there, in the dirt road only feet from his head, he could see a carriage attached to four enormous horses. The horses were stomping their hooves as if they were anxious to get moving, but the carriage was clearly parked because standing on one side of it Auggie could see three British soldiers.

He did not even have time to be afraid, because as soon as he saw them he felt the tingling. Not the light, skin-deep tingling he had felt the night he found the hole in the curtain. This was a deeper tingling, one that he felt throughout his whole body all the way into his bones.

Auggie looked all around until he saw what he was looking for: a small, pea-sized hole. He was familiar by now with the shape of such holes, with the darkness at their centers, and even with the tingling in his body that they produced. But it was the location of this particular hole that stunned him: it was on the side of the carriage, near the door handle, partially hidden by the flaking black paint.

He knew he had to move quickly if he was to use the hole before the soldiers rode away in the carriage. But he also knew that if he was captured, his chance to use the hole would disappear forever and he would be stuck here at the mercy not only of the British soldiers, but of Mr. Coyote as well.

So Auggie used a plan that he had seen work many times in the movies but that he never would have believed he would use himself: he picked up a rock, emerged from behind the bush, cocked his arm behind him, and threw the rock as far as he could into the woods on the opposite side of the road.

It worked. He couldn't believe it, but it worked. Just as he had hoped, the British soldiers ran in the direction he had thrown the rock. As they did, Auggie lunged toward the carriage and began scraping away the paint on the side of the carriage. Scraping and scraping and scraping until the hole was big enough to squeeze through.

He took a deep breath and, just as he could hear footsteps coming around to his side of the carriage, he stuck his head and arms through the hole and pulled his entire body into it.

He had escaped, but he had no time to savor his victory or to feel relief, because once he got through the hole and opened his eyes he found himself in one of the most awkward places of all: he was standing on the stage of the cafeteria at his school and looking out at the entire school—all the teachers, all the students, and all the specialists. Even the custodian was there.

And they were all silently staring at him.

Chapter 7: The Academy
Or, why philosophers have never been boring

Auggie stood there for a moment, unsure what to do. He looked out at all the faces staring at him. Some looked bored and distracted, but most looked at him expectantly, as if they were waiting for him to do something. But Auggie had no idea what he was supposed to do.

He stood there in his snow pants and parka, with the metal container from Mr. Jefferson tucked under his right arm and his left hand clutched around the headlamp he had stuffed back into the pocket of his parka. His fingers were still sore from tearing away the hole in the carriage, and his heart was still pounding from the excitement of escaping from the British soldiers.

Whatever this audience expected, Auggie doubted that he was the one who could provide it to them.

Just as he was about to turn and slip behind the curtain to escape the audience's gaze, Auggie heard the school principal addressing the audience. He looked down the stage to his left and could see her: standing there with a microphone and making an announcement to the entire school.

"Won't you all join me in welcoming our newest student, Auggie Spinoza. Auggie is an accomplished musician and will sing for us a very special version of the Star-Spangled Banner."

Auggie was baffled. *Him*, an accomplished musician? He was no such thing. He knew how to play the piano, and he liked to listen to music, but he wasn't what you would call an accomplished musician. And for that matter, he didn't really even know how to sing.

This did not seem like the time or the place to explain such a thing. If singing the Star-Spangled Banner would satisfy this audience and keep them from wondering why he was wearing snow pants and a parka to school, let alone how he had magically appeared on the stage clutching a special container, Auggie was willing to do it.

Just three days ago, it would not have been this easy. He would have been nervous and afraid. He probably would have pretended to have a sore throat. But Auggie was not the same kid that he was three days ago. He had met Charles Darwin and Thomas Jefferson. He had battled Mr. Coyote and Mrs. Peppersnell. He had escaped from British soldiers.

Compared to all that, singing in front of an audience seemed like a piece of cake. So he took the microphone from the principal and he sang. He didn't sing in his usual quiet voice, he sang hard and he sang loud. He sang like he had never sung before. And somehow, it seemed to work.

He could see the audience smiling at him. Some of them held their hands over their chests. And far in the back he could see Oliver mouthing the words along with him, a smile on his face, and one hand raised in the air with a thumbs-up sign.

When he finished, the principal thanked him and patted him on the back. "Thank you so much Auggie. That was wonderful."

When the assembly was over, Auggie joined Oliver and walked back to what he assumed was his classroom. At least, it had been his classroom three days ago. He wasn't sure what to expect now. But he wasn't really thinking about that, because what he was really thinking about was that container. What was inside it?

Auggie spent most of the school day waiting for a moment of privacy so he could find out what was in the container. He waited through social studies class and through read to self. He waited through Spanish and through music. He waited through lunchtime in the cafeteria, where he stared at his pizza and tater tots without eating.

He waited and waited and waited.

Just three days ago, he would not have been able to stand waiting for so long. But Auggie was getting used to waiting. Waiting just seemed like part of the routine to him.

Finally, it was recess time. Some kids rushed to play football or wall ball or basketball. Other kids went directly to the play structure and began climbing. Auggie didn't do any of those things. He went to the most secluded part of the playground, beneath the play structure that nobody ever used, and sat on the bark chips to examine Mr. Jefferson's container.

Even in the shade of the play structure, the gold of the container sparkled like sunlight reflected on water. Auggie wondered if it was real gold. He had only seen one other thing sparkle like this in his entire life: the shiny gold foil wrapping paper on the present he had never had a chance to open.

The container had an inscription on the outside that, as far as Auggie could tell, was the same inscription on the pouch they had found along Mr. Darwin's path: "Athena's smile is pure perfection, but the key to wisdom lies in reflection."

Auggie opened the clasp that held the lid tight on the

container and slowly opened it. There were three things inside the container. Two of the things were the same: they were metal rods about the size of crayons, but instead of a pointed tip each had a series of notches carved into the metal at one end and at the other end each had a small piece of stone the size of a small button. The metal rods were wrapped together in a single piece of paper which, when Auggie looked closely, he discovered was actually a hand written letter.

Fortunately, the letter was not in Greek but in English. Auggie examined it carefully and began to read:

> *Young Mr. Jefferson,*
>
> *I have greatly enjoyed your many visits and have learned much from our conversations. I share your love of philosophy and your admiration for our architecture.*
>
> *I fear that one day it may become necessary to close the holes in time forever. There is a way to do so, but I have scattered the clues among several different people.*
>
> *Within this box, you will find two keys. They fit the locks at the base of two columns of a building within the city of Athens. You will know the location of this building because we visited it together many times. It contains many columns. Only two of the columns contain locks that these keys will fit.*
>
> *In the same location, there is a third lock. I have given the key to this lock to another time traveler. You will need all three keys to gain entrance to the doorway you must travel through.*
>
> *Where the locks are is for you to discover. I can give you only a few clues. Together, the three locks form a most perfect shape. To discover what shape that is, you'll need to decipher this code:*

2Q53L1T2R1L   TR31NGL2

Once you have all three keys and have solved the code, you must go to the location of the locks. There, you will figure out where to insert the keys. And don't forget one final thing: Athena's smile is pure perfection, but the key to wisdom lies in reflection.

Your friend and teacher,
Socrates

Auggie read the letter at least three times. He recognized the name 'Socrates' right away; his dad had told him all about the famous Greek philosopher. He remembered his dad saying that Socrates lived in ancient Athens and was one of the most important philosophers of all time, even though he never wrote anything down.

Auggie remembered always thinking this was odd. How could you be an important philosopher and never write anything down? When he asked his dad, all his dad said was that Socrates had had many students and that those students had written a lot of things down. He listed Plato and a few other Greek names that Auggie didn't remember, and then he said with a twinkle in his eye and a wink: "And quite a few more names throughout history that you would recognize."

It didn't make sense to Auggie at the time, but now he understood. Many of the famous people he had heard of, like Charles Darwin and Thomas Jefferson, must have been Time Watchers who crawled back in time and met Socrates. He wondered if he would ever crawl back in time and meet Socrates.

He didn't spend much time wondering, though, because he was anxious to examine the code in the letter. He thought this was a code he could probably crack. But as he began to look at the code carefully, he was interrupted by a whistle.

Recess was over. He would have to crack the code later.

As he returned to his classroom, Auggie began to wonder when he would find the next hole in time. Even more than that, he wondered if Emily would be there the next time he crawled through time. Then he began to wonder something more frightening: would Mr. Coyote and Mrs. Peppersnell be there, too?

It would not take long for him to find out.

After their spelling test, Auggie's class walked to the gym for PE class. Auggie loved PE class. He loved to run and jump and exercise. He loved to learn new skills and play football and basketball and soccer. He even loved jumping jacks and push-ups and situps. He loved everything about PE class.

Except for Jerry Pipersnootle. Everyone called him JP for short. JP was not one of the nice kids. In fact, he was sort of a bully. He was good at sports, sure. But there were a lot of kids who were good at sports, and most of them were nice. Not JP. He liked to show off, he liked to taunt the other students, and sometimes he even liked to shove and push and hit when the PE teacher wasn't looking.

Most of the time, Auggie avoided JP. And when he couldn't avoid him he ignored him. That's what his dad had told him to do about bullies: ignore them. Because all they really want is attention, and if you give them attention they'll keep acting like bullies.

But today, Auggie could not avoid JP. And it was hard to ignore him, because the PE teacher assigned him as Auggie's partner.

"JP, this is a new student named Auggie. Why don't you make him feel welcome," the PE teacher said as she pointed to Auggie.

Auggie could see an evil sort of grin creep over JP's

face. Clearly, his version of making Auggie feel welcome was not the same as the PE teacher's version. He probably had a lot of things in mind that the PE teacher could not have imagined as he began to show Auggie around the gym.

Normally, Auggie would have been uncomfortable and nervous about what JP was planning. But right now, it didn't seem to matter. It wasn't that he was braver than he used to be. And it wasn't that he had a plan to prevent JP from bothering him. No, it was something else.

It was the tingling.

He felt it as soon as JP pointed to the blue exercise ball they used to practice balance exercises. As JP walked away toward the other side of the gym, Auggie could see a speck of darkness against the bright royal blue of the exercise ball. It was not a speck of dirt and it was not a speck of black paint. It was too dark for that.

It was a hole in time. Auggie was sure of it. He ignored JP and headed straight for the blue ball. The tingling was stronger now. It was in his head and his toes and his fingers and his bones. It was so overwhelming he thought for a minute he might faint. But he knew that he couldn't faint, that he needed to make it through that hole if he was to have any hope of ever seeing Emily or his parents again.

He also knew that he needed to act quickly. The PE teacher was talking to the class at the other end of the gym. JP was walking toward her, with his back turned to Auggie. Auggie knew that he had only seconds. So he grabbed the ball, poked his finger in the hole, and began to tear. He could feel the rubber stretching in his hands as he tore away chunks and chunks of the ball.

He was getting good at this.

In only a few seconds, he had torn a hole large enough

[141]

to crawl through. He took a deep breath and reached both arms into the hole. He paused for a moment and, just as he was sticking his head into the hole, he could hear JP's footsteps coming toward him.

The footsteps were getting closer and closer as he pulled his torso, his hips, and then his legs through the hole. He could feel a hand grasp his left foot as he tried to pull it through the hole. He kicked at the hand with his right foot and could hear a muffled scream as his left foot came loose and he was free of JP's grip and all the way through the hole.

He heard her before he saw her.

"We have to stop meeting like this," said a voice from behind him.

Auggie turned to see Emily standing behind him. She was wearing some sort of cream-colored robe over her clothing. She handed him the same kind of robe. "Here, put this on. It's a toga. It's what they wear here. I got these off of a clothesline."

As he slipped the toga over his head, Auggie looked around. They stood next to a small stone building set on the edge of a flat, open, grassy area that was surrounded by a sparse forest of trees. In the grassy area was a collection of stones of different sizes that looked like they had been fashioned into benches or chairs of some sort.

"Do you know where we are?" Auggie asked.

"Not sure when, but I think I know where. I think we're somewhere in ancient Greece. That explains the togas. Plus, the buildings that I've seen look just like pictures of ancient Greek buildings that we studied in school. Except for those buildings had mostly collapsed or fallen apart. A lot of these buildings look brand-new to me."

Auggie was anxious to tell Emily about the container and the letter inside it. He showed her the box and the metal rods, and then they sat on one of the stone benches and read the letter together. They looked carefully at the last line, written in code:

2Q53L1T2R1L   TR31NGL2

"Well, at least it's not in Greek. But do you think we can solve that code?"

"I think so. I didn't have much time to look at it before, but it looks like a pretty simple numerical code. It looks like he has just replaced each letter of the alphabet with a number. The trick will be figuring out what letter each of these numbers stands for."

Auggie stared at it for a moment until suddenly it felt like an e-mail was delivered to his brain. They had studied a code just like this in cryptography camp. It was a simple vowel-number substitution code.

"I've got it. He has just substituted numbers for each of the vowels. We just have to figure out which number corresponds to which vowel. I think he has just numbered them in order, so A=1, E=2, I=3, O=4, and U=5. Let's try that."

"Okay, so if we substitute A every place there is a 1, and an E every place there is a 2, and so on, we end up with this." Emily held out the piece of paper and showed him what she had written:

EQUILATERAL TRIANGLE

"That must be it," Auggie said. "An equilateral triangle is a most perfect shape. All the sides are equal, and all the angles are equal. How much more perfect could it be?"

Emily was about to respond when a voice from behind them interrupted her. They turned to see a large group of men and boys in togas and sandals standing around the remaining benches and rocks. Auggie had not even heard them walk up, and he wasn't sure how much of his conversation with Emily they had heard.

One of them had stepped forward and was looking at Auggie and Emily as he spoke.

"I see we have some new students, and they have started without us."

Students? Auggie thought he'd just escaped from school, and this did not look like any school he had ever seen before.

"I don't think we've seen you here at the Academy before, have we?" the man asked them politely. He was short and portly, with a bald head and a full white beard that looked like it could use a trim. "My name is Plato. Welcome to my Academy. We were just about to discuss the nature of happiness and wisdom. Would you like to join us?"

Auggie was too stunned to speak. Standing before him was one of the most famous philosophers of all time. Auggie had seen all his books stacked up in his dad's office upstairs, and he had seen many more of his books along the shelves of his dad's bookstore. He knew that his dad had spent hours and hours and hours reading Plato's books.

He knew something else, as well: Plato had lived in Athens in the fifth century B.C.E., which means they had traveled back in time something like 2500 years.

Turning all this over in his mind prevented Auggie from saying anything. He was speechless.

Fortunately, Emily was not so shy. "Hello there, I'm Emily and this is Auggie. We would love to join you. What should we talk about?"

"Well, my student Aristotle here spent a good deal of time yesterday talking about the nature of happiness." Plato pointed to a smiling young boy who looked like he was not that much older than Auggie. "What do you think is the key to happiness?"

"Well, I've always thought that the key to happiness is being true to yourself," responded Emily.

"And what do you mean by that?" asked Aristotle with a curious expression on his face.

"I just mean that you should stick to what you believe and trust your own mind and your own thoughts rather than being tempted or persuaded to think or do things that you don't think are correct."

"Yes, I agree with that. That is what we had concluded yesterday until Aristotle brought up a very important question." Plato pointed to a nodding Aristotle. "Aristotle, why don't you repeat the question you posed at the end of our session yesterday."

"Well, being true to yourself is important. But what if your beliefs are incorrect? What if you are wrong? Should you stay true to yourself and your beliefs if your beliefs are wrong?" asked Aristotle.

Auggie was no longer intimidated. He had finally recovered from his initial shock at being confronted with the philosopher Plato, and he knew as well that this young boy in front of him was also a famous philosopher. Or at least, he would be one day. For now, he was a student of Plato just like Auggie.

"That is a great question," exclaimed Auggie as Plato and Aristotle turned their heads in his direction, "that is why being true to yourself must be combined with reflection. Reflecting on your beliefs and opinions is a necessary part of being true to yourself. That's why I have always thought that reflection is the key to wisdom."

"So you mean that being true to yourself will lead to happiness only if you are also willing to constantly reflect on your beliefs?" Aristotle asked as he nodded his head.

"That's right," said Auggie. "You should always be willing to change your beliefs if reflection leads you to see that you are wrong. But once you have reflected, and you're confident in your beliefs, you should always be true to yourself. That's the key to happiness."

"That is a very persuasive argument, don't you think Aristotle?" Plato turned to Aristotle with a satisfied expression on his face, and he looked at Auggie and winked.

"I think I'm convinced," replied Aristotle with a nod and a smile, "but I'll think about it overnight."

"Quite right. I see the day is almost ending. We should begin our walk back to town before it gets too dark. Why don't the two of you walk with me." Plato pointed at Auggie and Emily.

As they walked slowly along a rocky path winding through groves of olive trees, Emily and Auggie could see ancient Athens spread out before them. They could see buildings made of stone blocks and columns, they could see people pushing carts, and they could see a bustling crowd in what looked like a farmers market.

Off to the left, they could see the Acropolis on a hill overlooking the city of Athens. They could see statues and monuments of white stone gleaming in the bright sunshine. Auggie remembered the Acropolis from his trip to Greece, but what he remembered were collapsed buildings and monuments of a dirty gray stone. What he saw before him was quite different: these monuments were beautiful and new. Some looked like they were still under construction. And among all that stone, what stood out the most was an enormous building that Auggie recognized well: the Parthenon.

"I think I know why the two of you are here." Plato looked each of them in the eye as he spoke. "We had hoped it would never come to this, but I'm guessing something has happened. The Great Battle Over Time and History is not going so well, is it?"

Emily and Auggie both shook their heads, surprised that Plato knew who they were and why they were there.

"Do you know where you must go?"

Auggie thought for a moment and then blurted out the only location that made any sense: "The Parthenon. But we don't know what to do there."

"That's right, the Parthenon. As far as what you should do there, let me tell you a story about my teacher, Socrates. As a child, he used to play up on the Acropolis, among the ruins of old temples that had been destroyed during wars that occurred before he was born." Plato pointed his arm toward the monuments on the hilltop. "None of these monuments existed at that time. These were built recently, after Socrates died."

Then Plato proceeded to tell them the story of Socrates and the beginning of the Great Battle Over Time and History. It began when Socrates was just a boy of 10 years old. He was playing one day among the ruins of the old Parthenon, which had been destroyed decades earlier during an invasion. All that was left was a scattered pile of stones, broken columns, and dirt. One day, he was crawling among the stones and beneath one of them he found a small opening that led him into a deep cave.

He could not resist exploring. As he descended deep into the cave, Socrates began to feel a tingling sensation in his fingers and toes. At the same time he noticed, even in the dim light of the deep cave, a tiny hole in the cave wall.

"Of course, we all know how he felt: he was curious, and he couldn't resist making the hole bigger and bigger. He chipped away at the hole until it was as big as an olive, then chipped away some more until it was as big as an avocado." Plato told them with an understanding smile. "He chipped and chipped and chipped until finally, the hole was big enough for him to crawl through."

The hole that Socrates had discovered and crawled through was the very first hole in time, and for many years it was the only hole in time. At first, only Socrates knew about it. He spent many days sneaking into the cave, descending into the deep darkness, and crawling through the hole in time. It was all very fascinating to him, traveling back in time and learning about other cultures and their history.

For years, Socrates traveled to the cave nearly every day. He used his ability to travel through time to gain wisdom, to improve his understanding of history, and to reflect on his current beliefs.

"You know, that's why Socrates always asked so many questions," Plato told them with an admiring grin. "He spent so much time studying other cultures and other periods of history, that he became skeptical whenever people seemed set in their beliefs or certain that they were right. He believed in reflection above all else. People were always annoyed by his constant questioning, but he really was just trying to get people to reflect."

Of course, Socrates was a philosopher. He sought wisdom

above all else. He had no thoughts of seeking power by changing history, or of profiting from his ability to travel through history. Eventually, when he began teaching philosophy to some of the young children in Athens, Socrates revealed his secret to a selected group of his students and they began traveling through time together.

"I was the first one he told," Plato said with pride. "And I'll never forget how shocking it was the first time he told me. And that tingling. Hard to get used to. Anyway, if Socrates and his students had been the only ones who ever traveled through the holes in time, everything would have been just fine."

"Let me guess: they weren't," said Emily.

"No, they weren't. Obviously, you know that by now. But you probably don't know how it all started. Socrates didn't realize how difficult it would be to keep the hole in time a secret. And the people who found out about the secret where the worst ones of all: the Sophists. Do you know about the Sophists?"

Auggie and Emily shook their heads. "No," they replied in unison. Auggie had never heard the word "Sophist" before, even from his mom or dad.

"Well, Athens has never been a very comfortable place for philosophers, despite what you might have heard. Socrates did not have many friends. The most powerful people in the city, and in fact most people in the city, were fonder of a group of people that we call Sophists. The Sophists specialized in persuasion, not wisdom. They often claimed that they could persuade anyone of anything, whether it was true or not. And usually, they could. The problem is that they used that power of persuasion to gain power and wealth. They were sneaky and clever and not at all good."

[149]

At some point, one of the Sophists followed Socrates and his students into the cave and watched as they disappeared into the wall. Needless to say, he soon told a few other Sophists and they began to sneak into the cave and travel through time themselves.

"You can't blame them for that, really," said Plato. "After all, they were tempted just like all the rest of us. It's hard to argue with that tingling."

Socrates quickly became aware of the possibility that the hole in time was dangerous. If the wrong people began traveling through history and trying to make changes, it could be disastrous.

It was around this time that the people of Athens decided to build a new Parthenon, right over the ruins of the old Parthenon. This seemed like a great opportunity to Socrates. He worked with the architects of the new Parthenon to make sure that the entrance to the cave was covered up forever. These architects went to great lengths to close off the entrance to the cave, and Socrates and his students were relieved for a time.

But it was too late. The holes in time began to appear everywhere, not just in the cave. And they began to appear to everyone who had ever traveled through time. Not just philosophers like Socrates and his students, but the Sophists as well.

That was when all the problems started.

Unlike the philosophers, the Sophists did not try to learn from history.

They tried to change it.

They didn't want to change it to make it better. They wanted to change it to increase their power. They thought that if only they could make the right changes in history, they would become powerful enough to rule the entire world. And the first thing they tried to do was make Socrates and his students, and all the other philosophers for that matter, disappear from history.

That's really when the battle started, when the Sophists discovered that very first hole and started traveling through it themselves trying to make changes in history. From that point forward, the Great Battle Over Time and History has really been a battle between philosophers and Sophists.

"So that's the same battle we're fighting in our time? So are you agents also?" Auggie asked.

"The very same battle. Except that I believe you now call our enemies Time Vultures instead of Sophists. That's a better description, but they're the very same kind of people. And no, we're not agents in the way that you are. It's not until later that a philosopher named Augustine will establish the I.A.I.P.H., as I understand it. That name might be familiar to you, no?"

Auggie nodded. So that was where his first name had come from, from a philosopher named Augustine who founded the I.A.I.P.H.. His parents must have met him. Auggie wondered if they were there when the I.A.I.P.H. was founded.

Throughout the battle, Plato told them, philosophers have sought wisdom while Sophists have sought power and wealth. The philosophers have tried to protect history to learn from it, the Sophists have tried to change history to gain power.

But the thing about Sophists was that they really didn't know what they were doing; that is, they didn't have the knowledge they needed to change history in ways that brought them power. But they kept trying. And the philosophers kept trying to stop them.

"We've been battling them ever since," said Plato. "In

fact, most of my current students in the academy are Time Watchers themselves. We spend a lot of our time traveling back in time to battle the Sophists. So far, we've been pretty successful. But I'm assuming that the two of you are here because the battle is not going so well."

"That's right. It's not going well at all. But we've been told there is a way to stop them once and for all. That's why we're here." Emily spoke with a firm hopefulness that Auggie hoped was not misplaced.

"There is indeed. And I can tell you a bit about that. We all had hoped that it would not come to this, but Socrates did always worry that when he opened up that hole in time it was like Pandora opening up her jar. Fortunately, we can put the lid back on this jar."

Plato hung his head in sorrow for a moment, and then told them what they must do.

Socrates was certain that the very first hole in time was the key to everything. If it was closed permanently, all subsequent holes in time would disappear forever. Or, to put it differently, they would never appear. That's the key to defeating the Sophists: closing up that very first hole in time.

Even though he knew of its dangers, however, Socrates could not bring himself to close the hole permanently. Instead, he worked with the architects of the new Parthenon to make sure that the entrance to the cave was covered. But he knew that one day, it may be necessary to enter the cave and close the first hole in time permanently. So, he designed a hidden mechanism for opening an entrance to the cave from within the Parthenon.

Then he did something else. He scattered clues and keys to the secret entrance throughout history, among the many Time Watchers who had already begun to visit him from the future. No single person had every clue or every key, because Socrates was not certain who he could trust. Instead, hints and clues to the secret were scattered in fragments throughout history. Various writers, philosophers, and scientists throughout history have known one or two of these clues, but no one except Socrates has ever known the entire secret.

"Even I don't know the whole secret," said Plato. "I know bits and pieces, but Socrates never had a chance to tell me the entire secret before he died. But I do know this: once you close that very first hole in time, you will defeat the Sophists once and for all."

"But how do we know what to do?" asked Emily.

"Well, there are three keys. You must have those or you can't succeed. It's just a matter of figuring out where the locks are that those keys are supposed to open. You'll just need to think about the clues you've uncovered so far. That's not something I can help you with. If you are meant to figure it out, you'll figure it out."

They were walking beneath the steep cliffs leading up to the Acropolis and the Parthenon, approaching what appeared to be the city of Athens and its stone streets and buildings. The blue sky was turning a pinkish-purple color as the sun began to set, and several puffy blotches of white clouds lay scattered high above them.

"One thing I can tell you, though: whoever enters the door to the cave will not be able to come out. Once the hole is closed, the door will seal itself shut and can never be opened again. That is why it must be a Time Watcher who enters. That way—"

Plato stopped in midsentence as Auggie grabbed his arm and gasped. Looking diagonally across the street, he saw a group of three people that made his heart feel like it skipped a beat. There, looking in the opposite direction but with their faces plainly visible, were the last three people in the world Auggie wanted to see: Mr. Coyote, Mrs. Peppersnell, and JP.

Auggie wasn't sure what they were doing here, but he guessed that it wasn't good. They wore togas and sandals and were carrying on a very animated discussion. They seemed to be trying to decide which direction to go. They were about to turn in the direction of Auggie, Emily, and Plato when Plato, sensing Auggie's fear, turned down a side street between two buildings and pulled Emily and Auggie after him.

"I take it you don't want them to see you. I can guess why. Why don't the two of you continue with your mission and I will distract them for as long as I can." Plato began walking back toward the street, then turned and looked over his shoulder at Auggie. "Don't forget, the key to wisdom lies in reflection. That was Socrates's favorite expression. Good luck!"

Chapter 8: The Key
Or, why words can sometimes trick you

Auggie and Emily arrived at the Parthenon just after the sun had set. In the fading light of dusk, they climbed the wide stone stairs leading to the front of the building. There, they stood for a moment among the stone columns that supported the roof. There were eight of them on the front of the building and more than Auggie could count on each side of the building, and they seemed to glow a bright white in the fading sunlight. They were the biggest and tallest stone columns Auggie had ever seen, and they seemed to support the stone roof of the Parthenon without any effort at all.

"Wow," said Emily. "I bet a lot of work went into this building. I wonder what it's for."

Auggie didn't have to wonder, because he knew. "This is the temple of Athena, the Greek goddess of wisdom. I think there is a statue of her inside. Let's go look."

They walked through two rows of columns and entered the main room of the temple, where they stopped for a minute, awed into stillness by what they saw. They stood before a long rectangular pool of water, surrounded on both sides by stone columns slightly smaller than those they had just passed through.

At the end of the pool, gleaming even in the near darkness, was an enormous statue of a woman. She wore a shimmering golden robe that flowed gracefully down her body and was decorated at the waist and neck with ruby red jewels. In her right hand she held a bright golden statue of some sort and her left hand rested upon a golden shield that lay on the ground. Her head supported a golden crown, studded with jewels, and a golden spear rested against her left shoulder.

Auggie had never seen anything like it. For one thing, the statue must have been at least 30 or 40 feet tall. It was at least as tall as Auggie's house, and his house was three stories tall. And for another thing, it was covered with gold. What looked like real gold, although Auggie couldn't say for sure because really, he had never seen a statue covered in real gold. But whatever it was, it sure looked precious.

And then there was that smile.

Despite the glimmering gold and shiny jewels on the rest of the statue, Auggie's eyes were immediately drawn to the smile on Athena's face. It was not the sort of smile you would get from playing a video game or even winning a soccer match. It was a different sort of smile, the sort you might get from knowing something important or from having a deep sort of wisdom. And it was the most perfect red color that he had ever seen.

They stood there for at least five minutes, just looking at it. There was no one else there. It was just Auggie and Emily and the enormous golden statue of Athena. They stared at her, and she stared back with her unblinking gaze. And her smile. Perfect, wise, and red.

Finally, Emily spoke up: "Okay, we're here. This is the location we need to be at. Now we just need to figure out where that cave is and how we get into it. Why don't we look at the clues we have so far."

"Well, the first clue we had was about the location: the Parthenon. So we've used that one already, and here we are."

"Yep, and then we have these three keys: the two metal rods, and this red stone." Emily pulled out the red stone they dug up along Mr. Darwin's path. It was brighter and redder and shinier than Auggie remembered.

"Okay, so those are the three keys that Plato said we need. We just need to figure out where the locks are. In his letter to Mr. Jefferson, Socrates said that the three locks form the corners of 'a most perfect shape', and if we cracked his code correctly, that shape must be an equilateral triangle."

"And we also know that at least two of the locks are located at the base of two columns in this building. Socrates said so in his letter. All we need to figure out is where that third lock is." Emily looked around them. The room was full of columns. They lined the reflecting pool and the back of the room. Finding the right columns would not be easy.

"Well, let's get started. I suppose it will be easier if we figure out which columns we need to unlock."

One by one, they began examining the base of each column. Starting at the floor, they ran their hands along the ridges and cracks of each column, looking for a hole so small that a pencil would not even fit into it. They looked at every square inch of the base of the columns. They looked at cracks and ridges in the stone. They looked at areas where small bits of rock had chipped off.

They looked and looked and looked.

It was slow and frustrating work. It took them nearly an hour just to examine two or three columns. At this rate, it would be morning before they finished, and the Parthenon would be crowded with people. Once that happened, it would be impossible to search for the locks because it would attract too much attention.

[157]

Not only that, the longer it took them to find the locks, the greater the chance that Mr. Coyote and Mrs. Peppersnell and JP would find them. And they couldn't let that happen.

They paused for a moment, sitting on the ground with their backs leaning against one of the smooth round columns. It had been days since they had slept. Neither of them had eaten since the day before. They were exhausted and hungry. Before long, without planning to and without even realizing that it was happening, they slept.

This was not a light sleep of a daytime nap. It was not even the sleep of a normal night. No, this was the sleep that comes from utter exhaustion, from complete fatigue, and from a sort of mental depletion.

It was the sleep of two agents who, as dedicated as they were, had no more energy left.

They awoke to a gentle breeze and the first rays of morning sunlight sneaking between the columns of the Parthenon. Auggie sat up straight, and then jumped to his feet when he realized what had happened: they had slept through the entire night. Soon, Athenian citizens would be arriving at the Parthenon and Auggie and Emily would lose their chance to find the locks.

They had no time to lose.

Auggie shook Emily awake and they spread the keys out before them. In the early morning sunlight, the red stone suddenly took on a new meaning. Auggie rubbed away the remaining dirt and held the stone up in the light.

It was the exact shape of Athena's smile. The very same smile on the statue that stood before them. And it gleamed a bright, perfect red.

Was that the third lock? Athena's smile? Is that why all the clues kept repeating the phrase "Athena's smile is pure perfection"?

Auggie wasn't sure, but he knew that the way to find out was to climb the statue and try placing the stone against Athena's smile. So that's what he did. Or at least, that's what he tried to do. He walked to the base of the statue and looked for a foothold or something to grasp that would help them climb up it. But there was nothing, and the glimmering gold was the most slippery thing he had ever tried to climb.

He spent nearly an hour trying to climb the statue, but without any luck. Exhausted, he leaned on the statue and faced the reflecting pool.

The view was stunning. The night before, in the dim light of dusk, the pool had been dark and empty. But now, in the bright light of morning, the pool was filled with the glimmering gold reflection of the statue of Athena. Everything in the reflection was perfect: the shimmering gold dress, the bright gold statue held in Athena's right-hand, the perfectly round shield, the sharp tip of the spear, and the beautiful gold crown on Athena's head. The reflection was as perfect and beautiful as the statue itself.

Except for the smile. The smile on the statue was the most perfect and bright red color that Auggie had ever seen. But the smile on the reflection was dull and empty. It had no color at all. It was a sort of hazy gray.

It made no sense. Why would the reflection of everything except the smile be perfect?

And then it hit him. That phrase, "Athena's smile is pure perfection," was always followed with another: "But the key to wisdom lies in reflection." What if "reflection" had two meanings? Not just reflection on our thoughts and beliefs leading to wisdom, but also the reflection in the pool, the reflection that Auggie was staring at, the reflection that he noticed right away was imperfect in only one way: the reflection of Athena's smile was not perfect.

Auggie knew immediately how he could make the reflection look perfect, and he suspected that was the third key. "Toss me that red stone, will you? I think I know why everyone kept repeating that phrase, 'the key to wisdom lies in reflection'. Reflection has a double meaning."

Emily tossed him the stone as he waded into the reflecting pool. The pool was about a foot deep, and ripples appeared along the surface as he slowly walked toward the reflection of Athena's face at the other end of the pool. The water felt cool against his skin as he bent over and reached his hand into the pool. There, on the floor of the reflecting pool, in the exact spot where Athena's smile should have been reflected, was a hole.

He was absolutely certain that it was not a hole in time. There was no tingling. And nothing about it felt all that special. This was a different sort of hole. It was a keyhole. And he knew that he had the key.

Careful not to drop the stone in the dark water of the pool, he slowly placed one hand against the hole on the floor of the pool as he reached the other hand in to insert the stone into the hole. It felt as if the stone was being pulled toward the hole, the way a magnet pulls toward metal. It fit perfectly, and as it snapped into place Auggie could see the red color of the stone illuminated through the dark waters.

The reflection of Athena in the pool now matched the statue perfectly. The dress, the shield, the spear, the crown, and now even the smile. Everything was perfect.

"Okay, that's one of the keys. Now figuring out which columns we need to put the other keys in should be pretty easy." Auggie waded out of the water and stood on the edge of the reflecting pool. "We know that this is one tip of an equilateral triangle. And we know that two of these columns are the other tips. How do we figure out which ones?"

"Well, we know that all the sides of an equilateral triangle are the same length, right?" Emily began walking toward the columns along one side of the reflecting pool as she looked around the room. "So I think the only possibility here is that one column on each side of the pool forms a corner of the triangle."

"Yeah, so all we have to do is figure out the distance between these two rows of columns. That'll give us the length of each side of the triangle. Then we can just figure out which columns are those exact lengths away from this first key, from Athena's smile in the reflection."

"Exactly," Emily said as she marched off the distance between the two rows of columns, pausing before she waded through the reflecting pool. "Okay, I came up with about 10 steps. Why don't I start at Athena smile, and walk out toward each column on this side until I find the one that is 10 steps away?"

So Emily waded back into the reflecting pool and began marching from the bright red reflection of Athena's smile to the row of columns. The first column she tried was only six steps away. The next was seven steps away. Finally, after several tries, she found a column that was exactly 10 steps away from the smile.

They bent over and examined the base of the column on the side facing the reflecting pool. It did not take long for them to identify a small hole, as big around as a narrow pencil.

Auggie pulled one of the metal rods from his pocket and inserted it into the hole. It fit perfectly, with a clunk and a snap as he set it into place.

Then they walked directly across the reflecting pool, 10 steps exactly, and found a similar hole in the column on the opposite side. Auggie pulled the other metal rod from his pocket and prepared to insert it in the hole.

"Let me make sure no one is coming before you put the last key in," said Emily as she walked toward the entrance. "Okay, coast is clear."

Auggie took a deep breath, paused for a moment, and then slid the rod all the way into the hole in the column. He felt a clunk and a snap, and then he felt something else: the column began to vibrate and shake. He felt it slowly turning around its center axis, like a giant screw being inserted into the ground. He looked toward the column on the opposite side of the reflecting pool. It was turning also.

The room was filled with light now as the early morning sun shone through the open entrance. Auggie and Emily could see both columns slowly rotating in place. The water in the reflecting pool began showing hundreds of tiny ripples. It felt as if the entire building was vibrating ever so slightly.

As the columns began to rotate more quickly, Auggie and Emily looked up at the statue of Athena. It was just as golden and just as large as before, but now something was different: it was moving. Ever so slowly, and without even a hint of a sound, the base of the statue was sliding along the ground away from them. It was as if Athena herself was taking a step back.

And then, as quickly as the rotating and vibrating and rippling and moving had started, it stopped. Everything was still and silent.

Auggie could hear his breath coming in and out of his nostrils and he could feel his heart beating quickly inside his chest. He wasn't sure why he was surprised by what he saw, but he was.

In front of the statue of Athena, in the floor where the statue used to stand, was a gaping hole as large as a doorway. It had jagged rock edges and a stairway leading down into total darkness.

It was the entrance to Socrates's cave.

Just as he was preparing to look into the cave, he heard Emily gasp. She was standing in the entrance, looking down the steps of the Parthenon. "Isn't that Mr. Coyote?"

Auggie rushed to the entrance and looked out at where she was pointing. There, about 100 feet from the stairway leading to the entrance of the Parthenon, was Mr. Coyote and Mrs. Peppersnell and JP. They were walking together, they were in a hurry, and they were coming straight toward Auggie and Emily.

Auggie knew right away that they needed to stop those three from entering the Parthenon. It wasn't just that Auggie and Emily were in danger, although they were. It was more important than that. If any one of those three entered the Parthenon, they would find Socrates's cave. And if they found that cave, they would find the original hole in time. Once they found that, Auggie knew, there would be no chance of stopping them and no chance of restoring history. If that happened, he would never see his parents again.

There was no time to figure out a plan, but Auggie had an idea. "I'll distract them. You go into the cave and complete our mission."

"But once I go into the cave, the door will close behind me. You'll be stuck here."

"Don't worry about that, I'll try to catch you before it closes." Auggie turned and ran toward the entrance. He emerged from between the outer columns of the

Parthenon and stood at the top of the wide stone stairway just as Mr. Coyote reached the bottom of the stairs. JP and Mrs. Peppersnell were a few steps behind Mr. Coyote, and all three froze in place as they saw Auggie at the top of the stairs.

He knew he had to act quickly. If any of those three entered the Parthenon now, they would have access to the cave. He couldn't let that happen.

Before Mr. Coyote had a chance to move, Auggie ran down the stairs two at a time, as fast as he could, heading diagonally toward the corner opposite Mr. Coyote. He reached the bottom of the stairs just as Mr. Coyote lunged toward him and nearly grabbed his toga.

Then he was free, running as fast as he could around the corner and down the side of the Parthenon as Mr. Coyote, Mrs. Peppersnell, and JP chased him.

Auggie knew that what he was planning was very risky. It depended entirely upon his ability to outrun the three people who were chasing him. He was confident that it would work because he knew that he was good at running. He knew that he was fast, and he knew for certain that he could outrun Mr. Coyote. He had done it before. And he was pretty sure that he knew he could outrun Mrs. Peppersnell. He had never actually raced her, but he had seen her running around the track after school and he was pretty confident she was not as fast as he was.

But there was something that Auggie didn't know, something that he hadn't learned in PE class or soccer practice or basketball games, something that would have been helpful to know before he came up with this plan: JP was fast. Not as fast as Auggie, maybe, but fast. Much faster than Auggie thought.

As he looked over his left shoulder and ran around the

back of the Parthenon, Auggie could see that JP was already far ahead of Mr. Coyote and Mrs. Peppersnell. He looked strong and full of energy. And he was getting closer.

Auggie stuck to his plan. This was no time to have doubts. This was a time to run faster. Faster than he ran when he raced Oliver to win the title of fastest kid in school. Faster than he ran when he scored his first goal in soccer. Faster than he ran the first time Mr. Coyote chased him. Faster than he had ever run before.

As he rounded the front corner of the Parthenon and approached the front steps, Auggie could see that he had left JP far behind. He could see Mr. Coyote and Mrs. Peppersnell far in the distance behind him.

But he could also feel the ground vibrating beneath him.

The statue must be moving, he thought to himself as he bounded up the steps two at a time and hurried into the main room of the Parthenon. He could see Athena's bright red smile reflected in the rippling water in front of him. He could see the two columns slowly rotating. He could see the statue of Athena sliding toward him, slowly but with increasing speed.

As he paused at the end of the reflecting pool, he could see one other thing: looking at him expectantly from the gaping hole that was slowly being covered by the advancing statue of Athena was Emily. She had her arm extended toward him and was motioning him to hurry.

Auggie wasn't sure he had enough time to reach the entrance to the cave before the doorway closed, but he knew he had to try. He darted around the edge of the reflecting pool in a full sprint and covered the remaining distance in only a few seconds. Soon, he was only a few steps away from the entrance. He could see the statue sliding faster and faster toward him. There was only a small gap between the statue and the edge of the entrance now.

It's now or never, thought Auggie as he dove toward the hole and rolled through the gap just before it narrowed to only a few inches. He was safe.

As he looked back and watched the gap close behind him, he could see the sunlight, the columns, and then, at the very last moment, when the gap was only an inch wide, he could see JP's outstretched hand reaching for the opening. But it was too late. JP and Mr. Coyote and Mrs. Peppersnell were stuck on the outside.

Chapter 9: The Return

Or, why every ending is also a beginning

Emily and Auggie sat motionless in total darkness for at least two or three minutes. They were locked inside the cave all by themselves. The only sound was the dog-like panting of Auggie's heavy breathing. It was cold, it was damp, and it was a little bit scary.

But none of that bothered Auggie because he felt an overwhelming sense of exhilaration.

That's all he could think as he sat there in the darkness: they had made it. As difficult as it had been, they had succeeded. They had figured out the secret of the keyholes arranged in the shape of an equilateral triangle. They had figured out how to open the entrance to Socrates's cave. They had even escaped from JP and Mr. Coyote and Mrs. Peppersnell.

Auggie was so exhilarated that he forgot for a moment that they had more work to do, that in fact they had not yet succeeded at all in completing the mission they had come here for. But it didn't take long for Emily to remind him.

"Hey, why don't you whip out that trusty headlamp of yours so we can see where we are going?"

Auggie pulled his headlamp out of his pocket and put it on his head. He turned it on to the brightest setting. Then he and Emily looked around.

They were in a narrow cave, perhaps 6 feet high and 6 feet wide. The walls and ceiling were made of large gray boulders and the floor was a mixture of dirt, gravel, and large stones. In the light of Auggie's headlamp, everything took on a gray brown color except every once in a while, when the light from his headlamp reflected off a sparkly rock in the wall of the cave, giving the walls the appearance for only a moment of silver glitter.

Before them, the floor of the cave descended at about the same angle as a typical staircase. They could see about 10 feet in front of them, but after that the cave disappeared into total darkness.

It was a scary sort of darkness, the kind that made a person want to turn and run rather than wade right in. Looking at it, Auggie was surprised that Socrates had been tempted to explore it in the first place. Especially when he was a kid, but even when he was a grown up. Auggie wasn't sure how Socrates had persuaded his students to explore the cave with him, but he knew that he was glad that he wasn't one of the students.

"I guess we should get going. Probably down there, huh?"

"How will we know where the hole is that we need to cover?" asked Auggie.

"I don't know. I think we'll know when we know. I suppose the tingling will help."

They moved slowly and carefully over damp and slippery rocks, descending into the darkness of the cave. After about 20 feet, the walls of the cave widened. Soon it was as if they were walking down a hallway at school, with walls spread far apart and the ceiling high over their heads. In some places, the floor of the cave was almost level but in most places it was at least as steep as a stairway.

They climbed down into the cave for what seemed like hours.

Auggie's legs began to ache with the effort of climbing downhill, but still they climbed. Emily was so exhausted that she nearly fell down at least a few times, but still they climbed. At one point, the walls of the cave became so narrow that Emily had to remove her backpack to squeeze through, but still they climbed.

They climbed and climbed and climbed.

As they climbed, Auggie could see the light from his headlamp beginning to dim. This was a sure sign that the battery was dying. He wasn't sure how much more light they had left, but he knew that if they did not find the hole soon the battery would die and they would be left in total darkness.

Just when he felt like he could climb no more, and as the light from his headlamp diminished to only a faint glow, Auggie began to feel the tingling. "Do you feel it?" He looked over at Emily and she nodded back at him, squinting against the glare of his headlamp.

This was not the weak tingling that he had felt when he first discovered the hole in the curtain. It wasn't even the strong tingling that he had felt when he climbed through the hole in the carriage.

This was a completely different kind of tingling altogether. He felt it in his skin and his muscles and his bones and even his teeth. But he felt it in his mind also. It was like his brain was tingling with a special kind of happiness that he had never really felt before.

Now he could understand why Socrates kept traveling back into this dark, wet, cold, and scary cave.

They stopped in front of a pile of rubble and stones stacked against the right wall of the cave. Above the pile, and about chest height for Auggie, was a perfectly round hole the size of an exercise ball.

[169]

Unlike the other holes in time that Auggie had seen, this one was not dark. Not at all dark. It glowed brightly in the deep darkness of the cave, like a small star in the emptiness of outer space, composed of a swirling mixture of every color Auggie could imagine, from red to orange to yellow to green to blue to violet, all churning powerfully within the hole. It looked, as much as anything, like a giant crayola hurricane.

And it hummed. Not the annoying hum of a machine, but a gentle soothing kind of hum. Almost like the lazy summer humming of bees around a fruit tree, but softer and quieter. The sort of hum that made Auggie feel like he wanted to get closer.

They stood and stared at it for the longest time.

Auggie could tell that Emily felt the same sort of tingling that he did, that she couldn't stop staring at the hole any more than he could, and that she was tempted just like he was. He had not really understood what Plato meant when he talked about the temptation of the hole, but now he understood.

Even though he knew that what he needed to do was cover the hole, he felt an almost overwhelming temptation to ignore what he knew he should do and to do instead what he wanted to do. And what he wanted to do was to dive directly into that hole.

Emily was the first one to say something about it. "It sure is tempting to just dive in there, isn't it?"

Auggie nodded. It certainly was tempting.

He thought about all the different periods in history he would like to visit, about all the things he could learn from continuing to travel through time, and about how much fun it would be to visit the Vikings or ancient Rome or Napoleon.

[170]

But then he thought about his home. His room, which he had decorated a few years ago with Star Wars and Lord of the Rings posters. His yard, with the soccer goal at one end and the basketball hoop at the other. The family room, with cupboards full of games and toys and Legos and coloring books.

Most of all, he thought about his family. His mom, his dad, and his sister. If he did not complete this mission, they would be gone forever. Closing up this hole in time was the only chance he had of ever seeing them again.

So as tempted as he was, he did what he knew was the right thing. He stayed true to himself. "Tempting, yes. But we need to cover it up anyway, don't we?"

Emily looked at him and nodded. He could tell by looking in her eyes that she had been thinking the same thoughts that he had. Temptation followed by the realization that the right thing to do was to close up the hole.

Without any further hesitation, they bent over the pile of stones and rubble and one by one began placing the stones in the hole. Had these been ordinary stones, it would have been quite a challenge to pile them in a hole and expect them to stay there.

But these were not ordinary stones.

Auggie could tell when he picked up the first stone that there was something different about these stones. They were sticky. And light. Like stones made out of squished-up cotton candy. When Auggie and Emily placed them around the edges of the hole, they stuck there and then gradually seemed to become a part of the rock wall. It was a little strange, like watching a rock wall grow.

The light from Auggie's headlamp was completely gone now, and the only light in the cave came from the hole itself. Soon, they had reduced the hole to the size of a watermelon. Then, it was the size of a soccer ball. Finally, it was down to the size of a baseball and Auggie held the last baseball-sized stone in his right hand.

"What do you think will happen to us when we close up the hole?" he asked Emily.

"I don't know. I think that's what Plato was trying to tell us before we got interrupted. I suppose if we close this hole, and none of the other holes ever appear from now into the future, it will be as if none of us ever traveled through time. Not you and me, not our parents, not anyone."

"So that will mean that none of the changes that the Time Vultures made will ever have actually happened, right?"

"I hope so. But I guess we'll find out, won't we?"

Auggie took one last look at Emily in the dim light of the cave, and then he took a deep breath and placed the final stone over the baseball-sized hole. It fit perfectly. As he felt it stick into place, he felt a momentary surge of tingling in his body. His heart began beating faster and his breath came in gasps. He thought for a moment that he might faint right then and there.

And then suddenly, as if a switch had been turned off, there was nothing. No tingling in his body. No light from the hole. No humming. Nothing.

Nothing but silence and total darkness.

Auggie stood still for a least a full minute. He couldn't see or hear anything. Finally, he called out softly to Emily. "Do you think it worked?"

There was no answer. Just silence and darkness.

Auggie cleared his throat and called out a little louder: "Emily, are you there?"

Suddenly, Auggie heard a door open and he was bathed in light.

"Augs, who are you talking to in there? And what are you doing in your closet, in the first place?"

It was his dad.

He was home.

And he was standing in the closet of his bedroom. It looked exactly as he remembered it, with clothes scattered on the floor and a few shirts hanging on hangers.

"Why don't you come downstairs, we're ready for you to open your birthday presents."

Auggie followed his dad through his bedroom, down the hallway, and down the stairs into the family room. Everything looked the same as he remembered it. The carpeting was the same. The pictures on the walls were the same. The banister on the stairway was the same. Everything was the same. Exactly the same.

It looked as if everything was back to normal. At least, it was normal in the sense that everything was in the right place. This was his house. This was his family. Everything was just as he remembered it.

But it still didn't feel normal to Auggie.

He wasn't sure how it could be that he had been traveling through time for several days now, but now it seemed like he had arrived back in the present exactly on his birthday, on the very day that his travels through time had begun.

He was trying to sort this out in his head when he entered the family room and was greeted with his mom's smile and a high five from his little sister. Now things were beginning to seem more normal to him. It seemed to Auggie like he had his old life back, the life he had before he found that very first hole, the one in the curtain. He felt

[173]

an overwhelming sense of relief as all the tension and fear and nervousness that he had felt over the last few days drained out of his body and was replaced with a contented but tired happiness.

Then he saw the stack of presents on the floor of the family room and he felt a cold chill enter his body.

Sitting on the very top of the stack was a present the size of a book, wrapped in shiny gold foil. It looked exactly like the present he had seen on the kitchen counter the night he traveled back in time. Exactly like the present that Mr. Coyote had stared at with such interest the very first night Auggie met him. Exactly like the present that Auggie had concluded must have contained the Agent Orientation Manual that explained how to travel through time and complete missions.

"Why don't you open this one first," said his mother as she handed him the present wrapped in gold foil. "Your father was excited to give you this."

Auggie was nervous. He could feel his palms sweating and his hands shaking. What if this was the Agent Orientation Manual? What if the mission that he and Emily just completed hadn't really worked at all? What if he had to continue traveling through time, completing missions and battling Time Vultures? What if he had to spend his whole life worrying that the Time Vultures might succeed and that his family might disappear from history at any moment?

It was too much for Auggie to think about, so he took the present from his mother and slowly tore the gold foil wrapping paper off of it, nervous and scared about what he might discover inside the package. As he removed the last bit of wrapping paper and stared at what was inside, he was stunned.

It wasn't an Agent Orientation Manual.

But Auggie was surprised, anyway. It was a book, and he recognized it right away. Or at least he recognized the author. It was someone he had just met. The title of the book was *The Republic*, and it was written by Plato.

"This is one of my favorite books of philosophy," his dad said as he pointed to the book. "There's a story in here about a cave, about a group of people who are trapped in a cave and fooled by shadows on the wall of the cave that they think are real. Even when a very wise man enters the cave and urges them to reflect on what they're seeing, they ignore him. It's a pretty famous story, but I've always wondered how Plato thought of the idea."

Auggie nodded and looked curious. Of course, he knew exactly how Plato had come up with the idea of telling a story about a cave. But he couldn't very well tell his parents that, because they would never believe him. And he certainly couldn't tell them that he had just met Plato the day before. They'd think he was crazy. So Auggie smiled and thanked them and then he opened the rest of his birthday presents.

The rest of the night was about as ordinary as all the nights Auggie could remember before he first started traveling through time. He ate dinner with his family, he watched his dad read a book on the sofa in the family room, and he talked with his mom about his homework from school. Just an ordinary night, or at least as ordinary a night as Auggie could imagine after the experience he had just been through.

For some people, ordinary might not be exciting enough. Some people might even think that ordinary is the same as boring or dull. Not Auggie. He had experienced enough excitement, fear, and uncertainty over the past

[175]

several days to last a lifetime. He didn't crave the exceptional or extraordinary or odd at this point, not after what he had been through. Not at all. What he craved above all else was just a typical, ordinary, familiar evening.

And that's exactly what he got.

The first chance he had, before he got ready for bed, he rushed to his computer to check his e-mail. He was curious what had happened to Emily, and he hoped that she had sent him an e-mail. When he checked, he found just one e-mail in his inbox, and it was from Emily Emerson. It was short and to the point:

> Auggie, I think everything worked. It's all normal
> here. Let's keep in touch. M & M

That night, as he lay in bed staring at the ceiling and preparing for the exhausted sleep of a retired agent, Auggie thought about all the places he had been and all the people he had met. He desperately wanted to tell someone what he had been through. But he knew that he could never tell his parents. And he sure couldn't tell his teachers. He couldn't even tell Oliver.

None of them would believe him.

He wouldn't have believed it himself until a few days ago.

He eventually decided that none of that mattered. He knew. And Emily knew. And now that they had completed their final mission, it didn't really matter that no one else knew. There would be no more holes in time and no more traveling through time. Everything was back to normal, and Auggie expected that it would stay that way.

Just as he was about to fall asleep, he noticed something strange on the ceiling. A small black speck. It wasn't a bug because it didn't move, and it didn't look like a piece of dirt either. Auggie stared at it for a moment before he realized what it was.

It was a hole.

A tiny, almost invisible hole. But definitely a hole. Whether it was a hole in time or just an ordinary hole in the ceiling, Auggie wasn't sure. And he didn't plan to find out. He rolled over on his right side, pulled the covers up under his chin, and went to sleep.

Made in the USA
Middletown, DE
28 January 2017